A HERO
OF OUR TIME

A HERO
OF OUR TIME

MIKHAIL YUREVICH LERMONTOV

TRANSLATED BY PHILIP LONGWORTH

With an Afterword
by
WILLIAM E. HARKINS

NEW ENGLISH LIBRARY
TIMES MIRROR

This translation first published in 1962
© The New English Library Ltd., 1962
Afterword © The New American Library of World Literature Inc., 1964

*

FIRST NEL MENTOR EDITION 1975

*

NEL Mentor Books are published by New English Library Limited from Barnard's Inn, Holborn, London, EC1. Made and printed in Great Britain by Love & Malcomson Ltd., Redhill, Surrey.

450022390

MIKHAIL YUREVICH LER-
MONTOV was born in Mos-
cow in 1814. A shy, awk-
ward, and ungainly youth,
he displayed precocious literary ability, and at sixteen, entered the University of Moscow. Two years
later, he apparently renounced his intellectual
leanings; he enrolled in a St. Petersburg military
academy and, upon his commission as an officer,
commenced a life of fashionable debauchery and
cynical amorous conquest. However, in 1837, a
poem attacking society as being responsible for
Pushkin's death revealed the true intensity of Lermontov's inner life and the measure of his poetic
genius; it also occasioned strong official displeasure
and brief banishment to the Caucasus. Upon his
return to St. Petersburg, his poetry and prose won
wide acclaim, his reputation reaching its zenith
with the publication of *A Hero of Our Time* in
1840. That same year, a duel with the son of the
French ambassador once more placed Lermontov
under official censure, and again he was sent to
the Caucasus. There, in 1841, a quarrel with a
fellow officer led to another duel. A single bullet
ended Lermontov's life at the age of twenty-six.

CONTENTS

Author's Foreword

The foreword is the first thing in a book. It is also the last. It serves either as an explanation of the work's intention or as a justification and answer to the critics. But readers are not usually interested in moral aims or journalistic attacks and so they do not read forewords. It is a pity that this should be so, particularly with us in Russia. Our reading public is still immature and does not understand allegory unless it finds a moral at the end. It cannot guess riddles nor appreciate irony; it is simply badly educated. It does not yet understand that obvious abuse can have no place in decent society and in decent books, that modern taste has devised a finer, almost invisible, but nonetheless deadly weapon, which, under a cloak of flattery, can deliver a well-aimed and irresistible blow. Our public is like a provincial who overhears a conversation between two diplomats from hostile states and believes that each of them is betraying his government for the sake of a tender mutual friendship.

Recently this book has suffered from the unfortunate belief in the literal meaning of words by several readers and even periodicals. Some were really terribly offended at being given an example of such an immoral fellow as the Hero of Our Time;

others commented ingeniously that the author had drawn portraits of himself and of his friends . . . an old joke and a sad one. But evidently Old Russia is made in such a way that everything in her renews itself without any equivalent improvement. Even the most magical of our fairy tales can hardly avoid the reproach of attempting an affront to personality!

The Hero of Our Time, my dear sirs, is simply a portrait—but not of a particular man; it is a portrait made up of the fully developed vices of our entire generation. You will tell me again that no man can be so vicious, and I ask you why, if you believe in the possibility of the existence of all tragic and romantic villains, can you not believe in the reality of Pechorin? If you admire far more unattractive and abnormal characters in fiction, why do you then show my hero less mercy than you show other fictional characters? Surely not because there is more truth in him than you like?

You say that morality cannot succeed from this? I beg your pardon. Enough people feed on confections and get bad stomachs. Bitter medicine—the caustic truth—is necessary. But when this is said, do not think that the author of this book ever had the proud conception of putting human vices to right. God deliver him from such indelicacy! He was simply pleased to describe a contemporary man whom he understands and who, to his misfortune and yours, is all too often met with. Let it be enough that the malady has been pointed out—God alone knows how to cure it!

Bela

I left Tiflis by post chaise. The luggage in my little cart consisted entirely of one rather small trunk which was packed half-full with travel notes on Georgia. Luckily for you the greater part of them had been lost, but the trunk with the remaining things, fortunately for me, remained intact.

The sun was already disappearing behind a ridge of snow when I drove into the Koishaursky valley. The Osset driver drove the horses relentlessly in order to reach the summit of the pass at Mount Koishaursky by nightfall and sang songs at the top of his voice. That valley is a glorious place! On every side there are inaccessible mountains, rose-red crags covered with green ivy and crowned with clumps of plane trees, yellow precipices, scooped-out hollows; and there, far, far up a golden fringe of snow, and below, mingling with another, nameless, stream, the Aragva gushes noisily out of the dense dark haze of a gorge and traces a silvery thread, sparkling like the scales of a snake.

We reached the foot of Mount Koishaursky and stopped by a tavern. A score or so of noisy Georgians and highlanders were gathered there; nearby a caravan of camels had halted for the night. I had to hire oxen to draw my cart up the damned mountain for it was already autumn and beginning to freeze—and the crest of the mountain was about a mile farther on.

There was nothing for it so I hired six bullocks and a few Ossets. One of them hoisted my trunk onto his back, the others began to help the oxen almost solely by shouting.

Behind my cart four bulls were drawing another with no apparent difficulty in spite of the fact that it was piled to the top. This circumstance surprised me. Its owner was walking behind it smoking a small Kabardin pipe worked in silver. He was wearing an officer's frock coat without epaulettes and a shaggy Circassian cap. He seemed to be about fifty years old: the swarthy color of his face showed that he had long been acquainted with the Transcaucasian sun and the prematurely graying mustache belied his tough bearing and sprightly appearance. I went up to him and greeted him; he acknowledged my bow in silence and blew out an immense cloud of smoke.

"We seem to be fellow-travelers."

Again he bowed without saying anything.

"Surely you must be going to Stavropol?"

"Yes sir . . . with government things."

"Please tell me why four oxen can pull your heavy cart without any trouble at all, while six beasts can hardly move my empty one with the help of these Ossets?"

He gave a sly smile and looked at me quizzically.

"You have not been long in the Caucasus, evidently."

"For a year," I replied.

He smiled again.

"Well? What of it?"

"It's this way, sir. These Asiatics are dreadful rogues. You don't suppose they're helping when

they shout? The devil only knows what they're saying. But the oxen understand them perfectly well.
You might harness twenty or more of the beasts to
your cart and they wouldn't move an inch while
the Ossets go on yelling like that. . . . The wretched
swindlers! But what can be done with them? . . .
They like fleecing travelers. . . . Save us from the
rogues! Look here, they'll try to get more vodka
money out of you. But I know them, they won't
catch me!"

"Have you served here long?"

"Yes, I was here in Yermolov's time," he answered, assuming a dignified air. "I was a second
lieutenant when I joined the line," he added, "and
was promoted twice in his time for action against
the highlanders."

"And what about now?"

"Now I serve with the third battalion of the line.
And may I ask what you do?"

I told him.

With this the conversation ended and we continued to walk side by side in silence. We found
snow at the top of the mountain. The sun disappeared as night follows day without a break as
it always does in the south; but thanks to the low
ebb of the snow we could make out the road easily.
It still went upward but not so steeply. I had my
trunk put back in the cart and the oxen replaced
by horses and looked down at the valley for the last
time. But a thick mist flowing out in waves from
the ravine enveloped it completely, and now not a
single sound reached our ears from there. The
Ossets crowded round me noisily and demanded
vodka money, but the staff captain shouted at them
so threateningly that they dispersed in a flash.

"What a people!" he said, "They don't know
the Russian for bread, but they've learned 'Officer,

give vodka money!' I think the Tartars are better; at least they don't drink."

The station was still over half a mile away. All about us it was silent—so silent that one could follow the flight of a mosquito from its buzzing. On the left the deep ravine grew blacker; behind it and in front of us the dark blue mountain peaks, furrowed with gorges and gullies and covered with layers of snow, were outlined against the pale horizon which still retained the last reflection of twilight. Stars began to sparkle in the dark sky; it seemed strange to me that they looked much higher than at home in the north. Bare black rocks protruded on both sides of the road; here and there bushes peeped out from under the snow; but not one dry little leaf moved, and it was cheering to hear, in the midst of that dead sleep of nature, the snorting of a tired team of post horses and the irregular jingling of a little Russian bell.

"The weather will be marvelous tomorrow," I said.

The staff captain did not say a word in reply, but pointed out a high mountain rising up in front of us.

"What is it?" I asked.

"Mount Good."

"Well, what about it?"

"See how it smokes."

And indeed Mount Good was smoking; light wisps of cloud were creeping up its sides and a black cloud lay on the summit, so black that it seemed like a spot on the dark sky.

No sooner had we made out the post station, the roofs overhanging the mountain huts, and welcoming fires shining ahead of us, than the wind blew damp and cold, the ravine started to hum, and a fine rain began to fall. I hardly had time to fling my cloak round me when the snow came falling down.

I looked at the staff captain respectfully.

"We'll have to spend the night here," he said vexedly, "you can't get through the mountains in a snowstorm like this. What do you think? Have there been any avalanches on Krestovoi?" he asked the driver.

"No, sir" replied the Osset driver, "but there are many just waiting to come down."

Because of the lack of rooms for travelers, we were led off to a smoke-filled hut to spend the night. I invited my companion to drink a glass of tea with me since I had an iron teapot with me—my sole luxury in traveling about the Caucasus.

The hut was built with one wall against a cliff; three slippery wet steps led up to the door. I groped my way in and stumbled into a cow (the cattle shed takes the place of servant's quarters with these people). Sheep bleating here, a dog barking there; I did not know what to do. Fortunately on one side a light was burning dimly which helped me find another opening similar to the door. Quite a memorable picture revealed itself here; the spacious hut whose roof rested on two sooty pillars was full of people. In the middle a little fire was crackling on the ground, and the smoke, forced back by the wind from the opening in the roof, spread around in such a thick cloud that it was a long time before I could see about me. Two old men, a great number of children, and a thin Georgian—all in rags—were sitting around the fire. There was nothing else to do so we took refuge by the fire, lit our pipes, and soon the teapot was hissing comfortingly.

"What pathetic people!" I remarked to the staff captain, indicating our grubby hosts who were looking at us in silence, in some sort of stupor.

"Extremely stupid people," he replied. "Would you believe it? They don't know how to do anything

—no capacity for any kind of skill! Your Kabardins or Chechens may be inferior creatures, cutthroats, or madmen, but these haven't even an aptitude for weapons; you won't see a proper dagger on any of them. The Ossets are a despicable lot."

"Were you long in Chechen?"

"Yes, I was stationed for ten years with a company in the fort there by the Kammenny ford—do you know it?"

"I've heard of it."

"Those cutthroats used to give us trouble, young man. It's quieter nowadays, thank God, but in the old days if you went a hundred yards outside the rampart somewhere or other a shaggy devil would be sitting, watching; you'd barely have time to gape and you'd get a lasso round your neck or else a bullet in the back of your head. Those were the days!"

"You must have had many adventures," I said, excited by curiosity.

"I can't say I didn't . . . There were times . . ."

At this point he began to tug at his moustache, hung his head, and fell into a reverie. I wanted dreadfully to get some story or other from him—a desire common to all travelers and writers. Meanwhile the tea was ready; I took two traveling glasses out of my trunk, filled them up, and put one in front of him. He took a sip and said as if to himself: "Yes, there were times!" This ejaculation gave me greater hope. I know that Caucasian veterans love to talk; they so rarely have the opportunity. He would be another five years with a company in some remote place, and for five whole years no one would say "hello" to him (because a sergeant-major always says "good day, sir!") And what wouldn't there be to talk about? When you think of the wild, inquisitive natives all around, danger every day, extraordinary happenings, you must regret that we commit so little of it to paper.

"Would you like some rum in your tea?" I asked my companion. "It's cold now, and I've got some white rum from Tiflis."

"No, thank you very much, I don't drink."

"Really?"

"Yes indeed. I have taken the pledge. When I was a second lieutenant we all got drunk once and there was an alarm that night. Well, we went to our posts tipsy and it was our luck that Yermolov found out about it. You can't imagine how angry he was! He was on the point of having us court-martialed. That's just it. Another time you'd go a whole year without seeing anyone but as soon as you touch vodka you're finished."

I almost gave up hope when I heard this.

"Yes, you take the Cherkesses," he continued, "they get drunk on their booze at a wedding or a funeral and that's when the slaughter starts. I had a narrow escape once and that as the guest of a friendly chief."

"How did that come about?"

"Well" (he filled his pipe, took a puff, and began to tell his story), "well, do you see, at the time I was stationed with a company in a fort beyond the Terek; I'd been there for nearly five years. One day in autumn a convoy arrived with supplies; an officer came with the transport, a young fellow about twenty-five years old. He reported to me in full uniform and announced that he had been ordered to remain with me in the fort. He was so slim and pale-looking that I guessed immediately he had not been long with us in the Caucasus. 'You have been transferred here from Russia?' I asked him. 'Yes, Mr. staff captain, sir,' he answered. I shook his hand and said: 'Very pleased to meet you, very pleased.

You will be rather bored here . . . er, well, we two will live here as friends. So please just call me Maxim, and, please—but why wear this full uniform? Always come to me in a forage cap.' He was shown to his quarters and settled into the fort."

"What was his name?" I asked Maxim.

"His name was . . . Grigory Alexandrovich Pechorin. He was really a very good chap, I can assure you; only he was a little bit odd. Well, for instance, after hunting the whole day in the rain and cold, everyone would be chilled to the marrow and tired out—but not he. Yet another time he would sit in his room, sniff at the wind, and assure me that he had caught a cold. He'd bang his fists on the shutters, then shudder and turn pale. Yet in my own presence he would meet a wild boar face to face. At times you couldn't get a word out of him for hours on end; on the other hand, occasionally, when he began to talk you would split your sides laughing. . . . Yes sir, he was a very strange man, but he must have been rich: he had all sorts of expensive things."

"Did he stay with you long?" I asked again.

"For about a year. I remember that year well too; he gave me some trouble I won't forget in a hurry! You know there are some people who are fated to attract all kinds of unusual things!"

"Unusual?" I cried with an inquisitive look as I filled his glass with tea.

"Well, I'll tell you. A certain friendly chief lived about five miles from the fort. His little son, a lad of fifteen, got into the habit of riding over to us every day for this or that, and we really spoiled him, Grigory and I. But what a little devil he was, as nimble as you please: he'd raise his cap at full gallop, or fire a rifle. He had only one bad trait: a terrible weakness for money. Once, for a laugh,

Grigory promised to give him ten rubles if he would
steal the best goat from his father's flock; and what
do you think? The very next night he dragged it
in by its horns. And when we took it into our heads
to tease him, his eyes would fill with blood, and
he'd go straight for his dagger. 'Hey, Azamat, don't
hang your head,' I would say to him, 'it's bad for
your brain-box.'

"Once the old chief himself rode down to invite us
to a wedding. He was marrying off his eldest daughter and we were his friends. One couldn't refuse,
you know, even if he was a Tatar. We went. A
crowd of dogs met us at the village with loud
barking. The women hid themselves when they saw
us; those whose faces we could see were far from
being beauties. 'I had a much better opinion of Circassian women,' Grigory said to me. 'You wait,' I
replied, smiling. I had my own thoughts.

"Many people were already gathered in the chief's
hut. You know the Asiatics invariably invite everyone they have ever met or come across to a wedding.
We were greeted with every respect and entered into
a pact of friendship. But I hadn't forgotten to notice
where they had put our horses, just in case of an
unforeseen circumstance, you know."

"How do they celebrate a wedding?" I asked the
staff captain.

"Oh, in the usual way. The mullah reads something from the Koran to begin with; then they give
presents to the young people and all their relations;
they eat, drink booze; then the trick riding starts and
some greasy ragamuffin will always mount a filthy,
lame old horse, show off, play the fool, and amuse
the honorable company. Later, when it has grown
dark, what we would call a ball begins in the best
room. A poor, old man will strum a three-stringed
instrument . . . I've forgotten what they call it—but

it's rather like our balalaika. The girls and young children stand in two lines opposite each other, clap their hands, and sing. Then one girl and one lad will come into the middle and chant verses to each other in a drawling sort of way, without any particular order about it, and the others take it up as a choir. Pechorin and I sat in the place of honor and, lo and behold, our host's younger daughter, a girl of sixteen, came up to him and sang . . . how can I put it? . . . as a sort of compliment."

"And what did she sing, do you remember?"

"Yes, it went like this. 'Our young riders are shapely,' she said, 'and their coats are faced with silver, but the young Russian officer is more shapely than they and the lace he wears is of gold. He is like a poplar among them; but he cannot grow or flower in our garden.' Pechorin got up, bowed to her, put his hand to his forehead and then to his heart and asked me to reply to her; I know their lingo well and translated his answer."

"When she had left us, I whispered to Grigory, 'Well, what do you think of her?' 'She's fascinating!' he answered, 'but what is her name?' 'Her name is Bela,' I replied.

"And she really was beautiful; tall and slim with eyes as black as those of a mountain chamois, which looked into one's soul. Pechorin, in a reverie, didn't take his eyes off her, and she stole a glance at him frequently too. But Pechorin wasn't the only one to admire the pretty princess: from the corner of the room another pair of eyes were looking at her, fiery eyes that did not move. I looked around and recognized my old friend Kazbich. He wasn't what you could call a friendly type, you know, though you couldn't say that he was hostile either. He was suspected of much but he wasn't seen to be involved in any mischief. He used to bring sheep to us at the

fort and sold them cheaply, only he never haggled; he
would not cut a price even if his life depended on it.
It was said that he liked to hang about with the
guerrillas beyond Kuban, and truth to tell, he had
the same scoundrel's ugly looks—small, dried up,
round-shouldered. And he was as cunning as a devil.
His long coat was always torn and patched, but his
weapons were silver. His horse was famous throughout Kabard—in fact, you couldn't imagine a better
horse than that one. Not for nothing did every horse-
man envy him and they tried to steal it more than
once, only they didn't succeed. I can see that horse
now: black as pitch, sensitive feet, and eyes no worse
than Bela's; and what strength! It could gallop for
twelve miles at a stretch; if it were left, it would run
after its master like a dog. It even recognized his
voice! He never used to tether it. That was a real
brigand's horse.

"Kazbich was more sullen than usual that evening,
and I saw that he was wearing a suit of chain-mail
under his coat. 'He's not wearing that chain-mail for
nothing,' I thought, 'He's up to something for sure.'

"The hut had become stuffy and I went out into
the fresh air. Night had already settled on the mountains, and the mist had begun to creep down the
canyons.

"I took it into my head to have a look at the shed
where our horses were, to see if they had fodder,
and anyway it never did any harm to be cautious.
I had a marvelous horse and more than one Kabardin had eyed it wistfully, muttering, 'Good horse,
very good!'

"I was creeping along the fence when suddenly I
heard voices. I recognized one immediately: it was
that scapegrace Azamat, our host's son. The other
spoke less, and more quietly. 'What are they jabber-
ing about,' I thought; 'surely not about my horse.'

I settled down by the fence and began to listen in, trying to catch every word. From time to time the sound of singing and the chatter of voices drifted over from the hut and muffled the conversation which I found so interesting.

" 'That's a fine horse you have,' Azamat was saying. 'If I were master here and owned a string of three hundred fillies, I would give half for your steed, Kazbich.'

" 'Oh, Kazbich!' I thought and remembered the chain mail.

" 'Yes,' answered Kazbich after a pause, 'You won't find his like in the whole Kabard. Once, beyond the Terek, I was riding with the guerrillas to drive off a string of Russian horses. Things didn't go well for us and we split up and went in different directions. Four Cossacks chased me; I could hear their heathen shouts behind me, and there was a thick wood in front of me. I lay forward on the saddle, entrusted myself to Allah, and for the first time in my life, insulted my horse with blows of the whip. It dived between the branches like a bird: sharp thorns tore my clothes, dry and twisted boughs of cork trees beat against my face. My horse galloped between the clumps, tore through bushes. It would have been better to have left him at the edge of the wood and gone in on foot to hide, but it was sad to part from him—and the prophet rewarded me. Several bullets whined over my head and I could hear the dismounted Cossacks running in our tracks. Suddenly a deep cleft opened up in front of me. My steed hesitated—and jumped! Its hind feet slipped off the opposite bank and it was hanging on by its forelegs. I threw down the reins and fell headlong into the gully. That saved my horse: it scrambled out. The Cossacks saw all this, but not one of them climbed down to look for me. They must have thought that I had fallen to my death. I could hear them trying to catch my horse. My heart was in my mouth; I crawled through the thick grass at the side of the gully and looked around. Several Cossacks were riding out of the forest into the open and my Karagyoz galloped straight toward them. They all went for him, shouting. They chased him for a long, long time and one of them in particular twice very nearly got a lasso around his head. I shuddered, turned my eyes away and began to pray. After a few moments I raised my eyes and what did I see! My Karagyoz was flying, flaring his tail, free as the wind and the heathens along way behind ranging across the steppe one behind the other on their worn-out horses. Praise be to Allah! That's the truth, the absolute truth! I sat in my gully far into the night, and suddenly, what do you think, Azamat? In the gloom I heard a horse running along the edge of the ravine. It snorted, neighed and beat its hoofs on the ground; I recognized the voice of my Karagyoz; it was he—my comrade. From that moment we never parted.'

"I could hear him stroking his horse's smooth neck and calling it all sorts of affectionate names.

" 'If I had a drove of a thousand fillies,' said Azamat, 'I would give them all for your Karagyoz.'

" 'No, I wouldn't take it,' replied Kazbich evenly.

" 'Listen a moment, Kazbich,' said Azamat, trying to flatter him, 'you're a good man, a brave rider, but my father is afraid of the Russians and won't let me go into the mountains. Give me your horse and I will do anything you want; steal my father's best rifle or saber for you—anything you like. His saber is a real miracle; put the edge to your arm and it will cut into the body by itself; even a coat of mail like yours won't make any difference.'

"Kazbich was silent.

" 'The first time I saw your steed,' continued Azamat, 'prancing underneath you, its nostrils quivering and sparks of flint flying from under its hoofs, something strange happened to me, and from that moment everything else disgusted me. I despised my father's best horses, I was ashamed even to point at them, and an intense longing possessed me; wistfully, I would sit on a rock for whole days and again and again your black stallion would appear in my thoughts, with its graceful step and its backbone as smooth and as straight as an arrow. It would look straight at me with its clever eyes as if it wanted to say something. I will die, Kazbich, if you won't sell him to me,' said Azamat in a trembling voice.

"I thought I heard him burst into tears; but I must tell you that Azamat was a very stubborn boy and even when he was rather younger you couldn't make him cry.

"Something that sounded like laughter answered his tears.

" 'Listen to me a moment,' said Azamat in a firm voice, 'I have made up my mind. If you like, I will steal my sister for you. How she can dance! How she sings! And she embroiders in gold—a marvel! No Turkish emperor ever had such a wife. If you want her, wait for me tomorrow night in the ravine where the stream runs. I will come with her by way of the next village—and she will be yours. Surely Bela is worth your steed?'

"Kazbich said nothing for a long, long time; eventually, instead of an answer he crooned an ancient little song under his breath:

There are so many beautiful girls in our villages,
With dark eyes that sparkle like stars.
To love them is sweet, a thing to be envied;
But gayer is the young warrior's freedom.

Four wives can be purchased with unalloyed gold,
But a spirited stallion is priceless:
It does not get tired by the storms on the steppe,
*Change will it never, nor ever deceive.**

Azamat begged him in vain to agree. He cried and cajoled and flattered him. Eventually Kazbich interrupted him impatiently.

" 'Be off with you, you idiotic boy. Where could you ride to on my horse? He'd throw you in the first three paces and you would break your neck on the stones.'

" 'Me?' screamed Azamat in a rage, and the iron of the child's dagger rang against the chain mail. A strong arm threw him off, and he fell against the fence with enough force to shake it. 'There's going to be trouble,' I thought. I turned toward the stable, bridled our horses, and led them out into the yard at the back. Two minutes later there was an awful hubbub in the hut. This is what had happened: Azamat ran in with his coat torn saying that Kazbich wanted to cut his throat. They all jumped up, grabbed their rifles—and the trouble began! Noise, shouts, shots. But Kazbich had already mounted and was turning round in the middle of the crowd along the road, waving his saber like a demon.

" 'A hangover at a stranger's party is a bad thing,' I said to Grigory taking him by the arm, 'hadn't we better save our own bacon?'

" 'Just wait a bit, it will soon be over.'

" 'Perhaps, but there'll be a nasty ending. It's always the same with these Asiatics—they get excited by liquor and there's a massacre!' We mounted and galloped off home."

* I hope readers will forgive me for putting Kazbich's song which, of course, was given to me in prose, into verse, but this is a habit—second nature to me. [*Lermontov's note.*]

"And what happened to Kazbich?" I asked the staff captain impatiently.

"What doesn't happen with these people!" he replied, filling his glass with tea, "He got away!"

"Wasn't he wounded?" I asked.

"God knows! But they are bandits as long as there's a breath in them. I have seen some of them in action, you know. For example, I have seen a man pricked all over with bayonets like a sieve and still brandishing his saber." The staff captain continued after a pause, tapping his foot on the floor: "I shall never forgive myself for one thing, though: I must have been possessed by the devil as we were riding back to the fort for I told Grigory everything that I had heard while I was behind the fence. He burst out laughing—he was a sly one all right!—he had thought up some scheme."

"What was that? Please tell me."

"Well, there's nothing for it, I suppose—I have started to tell you so I must continue.

"Four days later Azamat rode up to the fort. As usual he went to Grigory, who always used to give him sweetmeats. I was there. They talked about horses and Pechorin began to praise Kazbich's horse to the skies: how high-spirited it was, that it was as lovely as an antelope—well, really, the way he spoke there wasn't a horse like that in the whole world.

"The little Tatar's eyes began to sparkle, but Pechorin didn't seem to notice. I began to talk about something else but he immediately changed the conversation back to Kazbich's horse. This pattern repeated itself every time Azamat came. Three weeks later I had begun to notice that Azamat was turning pale and pining away from love like they do in novels. And what wonder? . . . Now I found out about all this later but Grigory used to tease him to distraction. On one occasion he said to him:

" 'Azamat, I can see that you have a tremendous liking for that horse and you will never see it any more than the back of your head! Now tell me what would you give anyone who would give it to you?'

" 'Anything he wants,' replied Azamat.

" 'In that case I will get it for you, but only on condition . . . Swear that you will fulfil it.'

" 'I swear—now you swear too!'

" 'All right. I swear that you will have the horse; but you must give me your sister Bela for him. Karagyoz will be a fair exchange for her. I hope you consider the bargain to be worthwhile.'

"Azamat was silent.

" 'You don't want to? Well, as you please. I thought you were a man, but you are still a baby: it's too soon for you to be riding.'

"Azamat flared up.

" 'But my father?' he said.

" 'Doesn't he ever go away?'

" 'That's true . . .'

" 'Agreed? . . .'

" 'Agreed,' whispered Azamat, 'but when?'

" 'The next time Kazbich comes here. He has promised to bring in a dozen sheep. The rest is up to me. You just see, Azamat.'

"And so they settled the matter—and to tell the truth it wasn't a very nice affair. Afterward I told Pechorin so, only he answered that a wild Circassian woman should be happy to have such a nice husband as him, for according to their custom he'd be her husband anyway, and that Kazbich was a robber who ought to be punished. Judge for yourself, what could I answer to that? But at that time I knew nothing of their plot. Well, one day Kazbich rode in to ask if we could do with some sheep and honey; I told him to bring them next day.

" 'Azamat!' said Grigory, 'Karagyoz will be in my

hands tomorrow. If Bela isn't here tonight you won't see the horse.'

" 'All right!' said Azamat, and ran off to the village. That evening Grigory armed himself and rode out of the fort. I don't know how they managed it, but they both came back in the night and the sentry saw a woman lying across Azamat's saddle with her hands and feet bound and her head wrapped in a yashmak."

"But the horse?" I asked the staff captain.

"I'm just coming to that. Early the following morning Kazbich rode up and drove in a dozen sheep to sell. He tethered his horse by the walls and came up to me. I entertained him with tea, because although he was a robber he was still my friend.

"We began to talk about this and that. Suddenly I looked. Kazbich had started. His face changed. He ran to the window but unfortunately it looked out on to the inner compound.

" 'What's the matter with you?' I asked.

" 'My horse . . . horse?' he said, trembling all over.

"Just then I heard the trampling of hoofs: 'Some Cossack must have ridden in.'

" 'No! I fear something bad, bad,' he moaned, and threw himself headlong out of the room like a snow leopard. With two leaps he was in the main compound. At the gates of the fort a sentry barred his way with a musket. He ran past the rifle and rushed up the road . . . Dust rose in the distance. Azamat was galloping away on the fast Karagyoz. Kazbich took his musket from its case on the run and took a shot. For a moment he remained motionless because he thought he might have scored a hit; then he screamed, banged his musket on the ground until he had smashed it to pieces, sank to the ground, and burst out sobbing like a baby. People from the fort gathered around him, but he didn't notice anyone. They stood there for a time talking and then went back. I had the money for the sheep put next to him—he didn't touch it but lay prone like a corpse. Would you believe it, he lay there till nightfall and through the whole of that night. Only on the following morning did he walk into the fort to ask people to tell him who the kidnaper was. The sentry, who had seen Azamat untie the horse and ride off on it, did not see any point in hiding the fact. When that name was mentioned, Kazbich's eyes lit up and he made off to the village where Azamat's father lived."

"What of the father?"

"Well, that's just the point. Kazbich didn't find him. He had gone away somewhere for six days. How else could Azamat have managed to carry off his sister?

"When the father returned, neither son nor daughter was there. He was a sly one. He must have known that he wouldn't keep his head if he were caught, so he disappeared. Most likely he joined some band of guerrillas and took his impetuous self off beyond the Terek or Kuban. Serves him right!

"I realized that I had had a big enough share in it already. So as soon as I found out the Circassian girl was with Grigory, I put on my epaulettes and my sword and went to him.

"He was lying on a bed in the outer room with one hand under his head and the other holding a pipe which had gone out. The door to the inner room was closed, and the key wasn't in the door. I noticed all this at once. I started to cough and tap my heels by the entrance, but he pretended not to hear.

" 'Mr. second lieutenant,' I said as sternly as I could. 'Can't you see that I'm here?'

" 'Oh, hello, Maxim. Would you like a pipe?' he answered, not raising himself at all.

" 'I beg your pardon. I am not Maxim; I am staff captain to you.'

" 'All right then. Wouldn't you like some tea? If only you knew how worried I am.'

" 'I know about everything,' I replied, walking up to the bed.

" 'That's just as well, I'm not in the mood to tell you.'

" 'Mr. second lieutenant, you have committed an offence for which I may be held responsible.'

" 'Oh, really? What's the harm? You know we've shared everything between us for a long time.'

" 'This is no joke! Your sword, if you please.'

" 'Mitka, my sword.'

"Mitka brought his sword. Having done my duty, I sat down by him on the bed and said:

" 'Listen, Grigory, you must admit that this isn't right.'

" 'What isn't right?'

" 'Your taking Bela off. That cheat Azamat! Well, admit it!' I told him.

" 'What if I like her?'

"Well, what could you reply to that? I was baffled. Nevertheless, after a silence I told him that if her father should start to ask for her she must be handed over.

" 'Not at all.'

" 'And when he finds out that she is here?'

" 'How will he find out?'

"Again I was baffled.

" 'Listen to me, Maxim,' said Pechorin, getting up, 'you're a kind enough fellow, but if we give the daughter back to that savage he'll cut her throat or else sell her. It's done now and you mustn't spoil things just because you feel like it. Take my sword and leave her with me.'

" 'Let me see her,' I said.

" 'She's behind that door; even I couldn't see her a little while ago. She sits in the corner wrapped up in a counterpane and doesn't speak or even look at anything; she's as timid as a chamois. I've engaged the services of our innkeeper's wife; she can speak Tatar and will get her used to the idea that she is mine, for she won't ever belong to anyone else except me,' he added, thumping the table with his fist. I agreed about this. What could one do? There are people with whom one must agree."

"And what happened?" I asked Maxim. "Did he really get her used to him, or did she pine away longing for home?"

"My dear fellow, why should she feel homesick? The same mountains were visible from the fort as from the village, and that's enough for those savage people. Besides, Grigory gave her a present every day: at first she refused the gifts silently and proudly, and so they fell to the lot of the housekeeper and excited her eloquence. Oh, presents! What won't a woman do for a colored rag! But that is by the way. Grigory fought her for a long while. Meanwhile he learned Tatar, and she began to understand our language. Gradually she got used to looking at him, at first from under her eyelashes or out of the corner of her eye, but she was constantly miserable. She would sing her songs under her breath so that it made me sad when I heard her from the next room. I shall never forget one scene: I was walking past and glanced in at the window. Bela was sitting on the stove bench hanging her head on her chest and Grigory was standing in front of her.

" 'Listen, my fairy,' he was saying, 'you know that sooner or later you must be mine, so why do you torture me? Is it because you are in love with some Chechen? If that is the case, I shall send you off home at once.' She gave a little shudder and shook her head. 'Or,' he continued, 'is it because I am completely hateful to you?' She sighed. 'Or does your faith forbid you to love me?' She turned pale and said nothing. 'Believe me, all tribes have the same Allah, and if he allows me to love you, why should he forbid you to return my love?' She looked straight at him as if astonished at this new idea; her eyes reflected disbelief and a desire to be convinced. What eyes they were! They shone like two coals. 'Listen, dear, good Bela,' Pechorin went on, 'you can see that I love you. I would give everything for you to be gay again; I want you to be happy; but I shall die if you are still going to be sad. Tell me, are you going to cheer up?'

"She became thoughtful and stared at him with her black eyes. Then she smiled caressingly and nodded her head as a sign of agreement. He took her hand and tried to persuade her to kiss him; she defended herself feebly and only repeated: 'Please, please, must not, must not.' He started to insist; she trembled and burst into tears.

" 'I am your prisoner,' she said, 'your slave; of course you can make me,' and tears again.

"Grigory banged his fist against his forehead and ran out into the next room. I went in after him. He was walking to and fro, sunk in gloom.

" 'Well, old man?' I said to him.

" 'She's a devil, not a woman,' he answered, 'but I give you my word of honor that I shall have her.'

"I shook my head."

" 'Do you want to bet on it?' he said. 'Within a week.'

" 'It's a bet.'

"We shook hands on it and parted.

"First thing next day he sent a courier to Kizlyar to do some shopping; a whole lot of different Persian cloths in uncountable quantities.

" 'What do you think, Maxim?' he said to me, pointing at the presents, 'will an Asiatic beauty hold out against a battery like this?'

" 'You don't know Circassian women,' I replied, 'they're not at all like the Georgians or the Transcaucasian Tatars. They have their principles, they are brought up differently.' Grigory smiled and began to whistle a march.

"And it turned out that I was right: the gifts had only half an effect. She became more affectionate, more trusting, but that was all. So he decided on a last resort. One morning he had his horse saddled, dressed up like a Circassian, armed himself, and went to her. 'Bela,' he said, 'you know that I love you. I decided to carry you off thinking that when you got to know me you would love me. I was wrong: Good-bye! You will become mistress of all I possess. If you want to go back to your father, you are free. I have done you wrong and must punish myself. Farewell, I am going—where, I don't know. I don't think that I shall hunt the bullets and saber slashes for long: then remember me and forgive me!' He turned away and put out his hand to her in parting. She did not take the hand, said nothing. Standing behind the door I could see her face through a chink. I felt so sorry—that sweet little face was covered with such a deathly pallor. Hearing no answer, Pechorin took a few steps toward the door. He was trembling, and do you know, I think he was in a frame of mind really to do what he was talking about in jest. God knows, he was that sort of man! But he had only just touched the door when she jumped up, burst out sobbing, and threw her arms around his neck. Would you believe it? Standing on the other side of the door, I cried too, that is I didn't really cry, but . . . it's too stupid . . ."

The staff captain stopped talking.

"Yes," he said afterward, twiddling his moustache, "I admit I was disappointed that no woman had ever loved me like that."

"And did their happiness last?" I enquired.

"Yes. She admitted to us that from the day she first met Pechorin he had often appeared to her in dreams and that no man had ever made such an impression on her. Yes, they were happy."

"How tedious," I cried in spite of myself. Indeed, I had expected a tragic outcome, and to be cheated of my hopes so suddenly and unexpectedly . . . "Well," I continued, "surely her father guessed that she was at your fort?"

"Well, it seems that he suspected. A few days later we found out that the old man had been killed. This is how it happened."

My attention was roused again.

"I must tell you that Kazbich imagined that Azamat had stolen his horse with his father's approval, at least I suppose so. Well, on one occasion he waited by the road two miles from the village. The old man was returning from a vain search for his daughter. His companions were lagging behind—it was dusk—he was walking his horse, deep in thought, when suddenly Kazbich sprang out like a cat from behind a bush, jumped onto this horse behind him, and with one blow of his dagger threw him on the ground, seized the reins—and made off. Several riders saw all this from a hillock; they gave chase, but didn't catch him."

"He had compensated himself for the loss of his horse and was avenged," I said, in order to get my companion's opinion.

"Of course, according to their lights he was completely justified," said the staff captain.

I was involuntarily struck by the ability of a Russian to adapt himself to the customs of the peoples among whom he happens to live. I do not know whether this attribute of mind is worthy of praise or blame, but it shows his incredible flexibility and the presence of a clear, sane intelligence which excuses evil everywhere where it sees its necessity or the impossibility of its destruction.

We had finished the tea in the meanwhile; the horses, long since harnessed, were chilled through; the moon grew paler toward the west, and I was already prepared to plunge into the black clouds which were hanging on the distant peaks like scraps of a tattered curtain. We went out of the hut. Despite my companion's forecast the weather brightened and promised us a quiet morning; dancing rings of stars interlocked in extraordinary patterns on the far horizon and, one after the other, went out as the pale reflection from the east spread over the dark lilac vault of the sky, gradually lighting the steep slopes of the mountains covered with virgin snows. To the right and left dark secret crevasses showed black, and mists, curling and twisting like snakes, crept away among the folds of neighboring cliffs as if sensing the approach of day and fearing it.

In the sky and on the ground everything was quiet, like a man's heart at morning prayer; only from time to time a bitter cold wind blew in from the east, lifting the horses' manes, which were coated with white frost. We moved onto the road. Five thin nags dragged our carts with difficulty up the tortuous road to Mount Good. We walked behind, putting stones under the wheels when the horses tired. The road seemed to lead up to the sky, for as far as the eye could see it went upward until it led into the cloud which since the previous evening had rested on the summit of Mount Good like a vulture waiting for its prey. The snow crackled under our feet; the air now became rarified so that it was painful to breathe; every other minute the blood would rush to one's head, but all the same some sort of joyous feeling moved strangely through my veins and somehow I was happy to be so high above the world; a childish feeling, I do not dispute, but being far from the conditions of society and much closer to nature, we cannot help but become children. Everything that has been acquired unnaturally falls away from the soul, and it becomes again what it has been and what it will surely be again. He who, like me, has wandered about deserted mountains and looked long at their fantastic forms and gulped greedily the life-giving air which fills their crevices, he, of course, will understand my wish to communicate, to tell, to describe these magic pictures. Well, at last we reached the summit of Mount Good and stopped to look about us. The gray cloud hung on it, and its cold breath threatened an approaching storm, but in the east everything was so clear and golden that we, that is the staff captain and I, completely forgot about it. Yes, *and* the staff captain: the feeling for the beauty and grandeur of nature is a hundred carat finer and more alive in simple hearts than in us, enthusiastic story-tellers with words and paper.

"You must have grown used to these magnificent scenes," I said to him.

"Yes, sir, and one can get used to the whine of bullets too, that is, used to hiding the involuntary pounding of your heart!"

"I have heard, on the other hand, that some veterans find that music pleasant even."

"Of course, if you like it, it's pleasant, but only because the heart beats faster. Look here," he added, pointing to the east. "What a country!" And really, I have still not, hardly anywhere, managed to see such a panorama as that: beneath us lay the

Koishaursky valley intersected by the Aragva and another little river like two silvery threads; a bluish mist crept along it, running away into nearby gorges from the warm rays of the morning. To the right and left, mountain ridges, each higher than the next, intersected and ranged beside each other, covered with snow and vegetation; in the distance there were more mountains, but no two peaks were alike and all the snow burnt in a rosy glitter so merrily, so clearly, that it seemed that one could live there for an eternity. The sun had scarely appeared from behind the dark blue mountain, which only an experienced eye could distinguish from the threatening cloud; but above the sun there was a bloody streak to which my companion paid particular attention. "I told you," he cried, "that there'd be bad weather. We must hurry or else it will catch us on the Krestovoi, if you please. Look lively!" he called to the coachmen.

They put chains under the wheels instead of brakes so that they would not slip, took the horses by the bridles, and started the descent. On the right there was a cliff, to the left an abyss so deep that a whole hamlet of Ossets living at its bottom seemed like a nest of swallows. I shuddered, thinking that often on a dark night here along this road, where two vehicles cannot pass, some courier drives through ten times a year without even getting out of his jolting carriage. One of our drivers was a Russian Yaroslav peasant, the other was an Osset. The Osset led the shaft horse by the bridle with every possible precaution, having previously unharnessed the leading pair—but our unconcerned Russian did not even get out of his driver's seat! When I remarked to him that he might well worry a little even if only on account of my trunk which I had no desire to climb into that chasm for, he an-

swered: "Oh, Sir! God willing we'll get there none
the worse: you know we aren't the first to make the
trip"—and he was right: we really might not have
got there, but all the same we did, and if people
thought rather more, they would be convinced that
life is not worth worrying so much about.

But perhaps you want to know the end of Bela's
story? Well, first of all I am writing travel notes,
not a story, so I cannot make the staff captain speak
before he actually did. So wait, or, if you like, turn
over a few pages, only I do not advise you to do
this because the journey across Mount Krestovoi
(or, as the learned Gamba calls it, "le Mont St.
Christophe") is worthy of your curiosity. And so
we descend from Mount Good into the Chertova
valley . . . what a romantic name! You immediately
picture a nest of evil spirits between inaccessible
cliffs—but it was not there: the term Chertova
valley is derived from the word *cherta* [line], not
chort [devil], because at one time the Georgian
border was here. This valley was walled up with
snowdrifts quite vividly reminiscent of Saratov,
Tambov and other *nice* places in our own country.

"That's the Krestovoi!" the staff captain told me
as we rode down into the Chertova valley, pointing
to a hill shrouded with snow. A stone cross showed
black on the summit and, barely noticeable, the
road led by it, passable only when the snow is walled
up at the side. Our driver declared that there were
no avalanches yet and to conserve the horses took
the roundabout way. At the turn we met five Osset
fellows who offered their services. Taking hold of the
wheels, they set about hauling and supporting our
carts, shouting as they did so. The road was really
dangerous. Piles of snow hung above our heads to
the right, ready, it seemed, to tear down into the
ravine at the first gust of wind; sections of the nar-

row road were covered with snow, which collapsed under one's feet in some places and in others had been changed to ice by the rays of the sun and the night frosts, so that progress was difficult for us: the horses stumbled; on the left there yawned a deep crevasse in which flowed a torrent, now hidden under a crust of ice, now rolling frothily over the black stones. We barely managed to get around Mount Krestovoi in two hours; not much more than a mile in two hours! Meanwhile the clouds dropped and hail and snow poured down; the wind broke through into the canyon and roared and whistled like the Robber Nightingale, and soon the stone cross was concealed by the waves of mist, each thicker and more oppressive than the last, which came in from the east . . . By the way, this cross has a strange, but commonly held, legend attached to it that Emperor Peter I erected it on a journey through the Caucasus; but in the first place Peter was only in Daghestan, and secondly, there is a large inscription on the cross saying that it was erected by order of M. Yermolov in 1824. But in spite of the inscription, the legend has become so established that one really does not know what to believe, especially since we are not accustomed to believing inscriptions.

We had to go on for another three and a half miles or so down the icy rocks and swampy snow to reach the station at Kobi. The horses were tired out and we were chilled to the bone; the snowstorm droned on more and more violently like our own north wind, only its wild tones were sadder, more mournful. "You are an exile," I thought—"crying for your wide-open steppes; there is space for you there to spread your cold wings; here it is narrow and stuffy for you, as it is for an eagle screeching as it beats against the bars of its iron cage!"

"That's bad," said the staff captain. "Look, you can't see anything anywhere except mist and snow; I'm afraid we'll be stuck in this hole, or else fall into a crevasse, and down there the Baidara is running too high for us to get across. That's Asia for you! You'd never believe there were such people or rivers!"

Shouting and swearing, the drivers were thrashing the horses, which snorted, resisted, and would not move for anything in the world in spite of the eloquence of the whips.

"Your highness," said one man eventually, "we won't get to Kobi now; won't you have us turn to the left while there's still time? I can see something there on the slope—it must be the huts; travelers always stop there in bad weather. They say they'll lead us to it if you give them something for vodka!" he added, pointing to the Ossets.

"I know, my man, I know without your telling me," said the staff captain. "Oh, these wretches. They're only too happy to find something wrong to get something for vodka."

"But do admit," I said, "that we would be worse off without them."

"All right, all right," he muttered. "That's guides for you! They sense when they can take advantage, as if one couldn't find the road without them."

So we turned off to the left, and somehow or other, after a lot of trouble, we reached a meager shelter consisting of two huts made of local stone and surrounded by a wall of similar material. The ragged proprietors received us hospitably. I found out later that the government pays and feeds them on condition that they take in visitors caught in storms.

"It's all for the best," I said, settling down by the

fire. "Now you will finish your story about Bela. I'm sure it didn't end there."

"And why are you so sure?" the staff captain answered, with a sly smile and a wink.

"Because it isn't in the order of things: what started unusually must finish in a similar way."

"Well, you've guessed right."

"I'm so pleased."

"It's all very well for you to be pleased, but to tell you the truth I feel sad to recall it. That Bela was a lovely girl. In the end I got as used to her as to a daughter, and she liked me too. I should tell you that I haven't any family: I've had no news of my mother and father for twelve years now and I never thought of getting a wife when I was younger—now it wouldn't suit me, you understand. And I was glad to find someone I could spoil. She used to sing to us and dance Lezgian dances . . . and how she could dance! I have seen the young ladies in our local society and once, twenty years ago, I was at a fashionable party in Moscow—but they came nowhere near her. Grigory would dress her up like a doll and used to tend her and cherish her; and it was a marvel how she improved while she was with us. Her face and arms lost their tan, and a high color played on her cheeks. She was so gay; she used to make jokes at my expense, the naughty child. God forgive her!"

"What about when you told her of her father's death?"

"We kept it from her for a long time until she'd got used to her situation, and when we did tell her she cried a bit for a couple of days and then forgot about it.

"Everything went beautifully for four months. As I must have already said, Grigory loved hunting passionately; he used to be in the forest chasing wild boar or goats and now he hardly ever went outside the fort walls. Well, I saw that he was beginning to fret again; he would walk about his room, his hands locked behind his back; once, later, without saying anything to anyone he went out shooting—and spent the whole morning at it; it happened again, then again, more and more frequently. 'That's bad,' I thought, 'something must have come between them.'

"One morning I called on them—I can see it now: Bela was sitting on the bed in a long black silk coat, pale and looking so miserable that I got frightened.

" 'Where is Pechorin?' I asked.

" 'Hunting.'

" 'Did he leave today?' She was silent, as if she found it difficult to come out with it.

" 'No, yesterday,' she said at last sighing heavily.

" 'Has anything happened to him?'

" 'Yesterday I thought and thought the whole day,' she answered through her tears—'imagining all sorts of misfortunes; I thought a wild boar had wounded him, that a Chechen had carried him off to the mountains . . . but now I think that he does not love me.'

" 'Really, my dear, you couldn't have thought of anything worse!' She burst into tears, then raised her head proudly, wiped away her tears, and continued:

" 'If he does not love me, who prevents him sending me home? I'm not forcing him. If this continues, I shall leave myself; I am not his slave—I am the daughter of a chieftain.'

"I started to talk her out of it.

" 'Listen, Bela. You know you can't expect him to stay here forever tied to your apron-strings; he is a young man who loves hunting—he goes away but he comes back; and if you are going to be miserable, he'll soon get tired of you.'

" 'True, true!' she answered, 'I shall be gay.' And with a laugh she took her tambourine and started to sing and dance and jump around me; but this didn't last long. She collapsed onto the bed again and covered her face with her hands.

"What was I to do with her? You know I never had anything to do with women; I thought and thought about how to calm her down and I couldn't think of anything. For some time we were both silent. It was a very unpleasant situation, sir!

"Eventually I said to her: 'Shall we go for a stroll along the battlements? The weather is marvelous.' It was September and really it was an extraordinary day, bright but not hot. You could see all the mountains as if they had been served up on a platter. We went and walked up and down along the fort wall in silence. Eventually she sat on the grass, and I sat down by her. Well, really, it's amusing to recall it, I used to run after her like a nursemaid.

"Our fort stood on a high spot, and the view from the wall was beautiful; on one side there was a broad plain, pitted with gullies and ending in a forest which stretched right up to a range of mountains; here and there along the range smoke rose from villages and droves of horses wandered about —on the other side ran a shallow little river, and the thick scrub that bordered it covered flinty heights which joined the main chain of the Caucasus. We sat at the corner of the bastion so that we could see everything on both sides. I looked out and saw that someone was riding out of the forest on a gray horse. He came nearer and nearer until he stopped on the far side of the river about two hundred yards from us and began to spin his horse round like a madman. It was very strange.

" 'Look there, Bela,' I said, 'you have young eyes. What sort of rider is that? Whom has he come to amuse?'

"She glanced over and cried out:

" 'That is Kazbich!'

" 'Oh, cutthroat that he is! Has he come to poke fun at us?' I peered out and it really was Kazbich, his ugly face as battered and grubby as ever.

" 'That is my father's horse,' said Bella, clutching my arm; she was trembling like a leaf, and her eyes sparkled, 'Aha!' I thought, 'the bandit blood speaks in you too, my dear.'

" 'Come here,' I told the sentry, 'examine your musket. If you unseat that young brave for me you will get a silver ruble.'

" 'Yes, sir, but he won't keep still.'

" 'Order him to,' I said laughing.

" 'Hey, my friend,' shouted the sentry, shaking his fist at him, 'just wait a moment, my little one, what are you spinning round like a top for?'

"Indeed, Kazbich did stop and began to listen; very likely he thought that someone was talking to him—how far from the truth! My grenadier took aim —bang!—missed; just as the powder in the touch-pan flared up, Kazbich nudged his horse and gave a jump to the side. He raised himself in the stirrups, shouted out something in his own language, bran-dished his whip threateningly, and took to his heels.

" 'You should be ashamed of yourself!' I told the sentry.

" 'Sir, he's only gone off to die,' he replied, 'you don't kill those damned people straight away.'

"A quarter of an hour later Pechorin returned from the hunt. Bela threw herself round his neck without a single complaint or reproach for his long absence. But even I was angry with him.

" 'My dear fellow,' I said, 'you know Kazbich was here just now on the other side of the stream, and we shot at him. Well, has it been such a long time since you came across him? These mountain people are vengeful. Do you imagine that he didn't guess that you had a part in helping Azamat? And I wouldn't like to bet that he didn't recognize Bela just now. I know that a year ago he had a tremendous liking for her—he told me so himself—and if he had any hope of raising a decent amount of bride money, he surely would have courted her.'

"At this point Pechorin started to think. 'Yes,' he replied, 'we must be more careful. Bela, from today you should not go outside the fort wall.'

"That evening I had a long talk with him. I was annoyed because he had changed toward the poor girl. Besides the fact that he was spending half the day hunting, his attitude had become cold; he rarely caressed her. She started visibly to pine away. Her little face grew longer, the large eyes darkened. You would ask her: 'Why are you sighing, Bela? Are you miserable?'—'No.' 'Do you want for anything?'—'No.' 'Do you miss your own people?'—'I have no people of my own!' For days on end you wouldn't get anything out of her but 'Yes' and 'No'.

"Well, I began to talk to him about this. 'Listen, Maxim,' he answered, 'I have an unfortunate character, I don't know whether it's my upbringing or whether God made me so. I only know that if I am the cause of unhappiness in others, I am no happier myself. Of course that isn't much consolation to them, but the point is that it is true. When I was young, from the very moment that I left my parents' care, I began to indulge furiously in all the pleasures I could get for money, and naturally these pleasures made me utterly sick. Later I entered high society and soon I tired of it too. I fell in love with society beauties, and was loved by them—but their love stimulated nothing but my imagination and self-love and my heart remained empty. I began to read, to study—learning also became wearisome; I saw that neither glory nor happiness depended in any way on it because the happy people are ignora-muses and glory is nothing else but success, and to achieve it one only has to be cunning. Then I became bored. Soon I was posted to the Caucasus; it was the happiest time of my life. I hoped that tedium did not exist among the Chechen bullets, but in vain, for within a month I was so used to their buzz-ing and the nearness of death that, really, I paid more attention to the flies—and life became more wearisome than before because I had lost my last hope. When I caught sight of Bela in her own home, when for the first time I held her knees and kissed her black curls, fool that I was, I imagined she was an angel sent me by a compassionate fate. I was wrong again; the love of savages isn't much better than the love of noble ladies; ignorance and simple-heartedness can be as tiresome as coquetry. If you like, I will tell you that I still love her, I am grate-ful to her for a few moments that were sweet enough, I would give my life for her, but—she bores me. I don't know if I am a fool or a knave; but what is true is that I deserve pity to a large degree, more, perhaps, than she does. I have a spirit that has been spoiled by the world, a disturbed imagination, and a heart that can't be satisfied; everything means so little to me; I get used to sorrow as easily as I do to pleasure, and from day to day my life becomes emptier. I have only one resort left: travel. I will leave as soon as possible, but not for Europe, God forbid. I shall go to America, Arabia, India—perhaps I shall die on the road somewhere. At least, with the help of storms and bad roads, I am sure that this last consolation won't be exhausted so quickly.' He spoke in this way for a long time, and his words stayed in my memory because it was the first time I had heard such things from a twenty-five-year-old man, and God willing it will be the last. What wonder! "Please tell me," continued the staff captain, turning to me, "You must have been in the capital, and recently too: can it be possible that the young men there are all the same?"

I replied that many people were saying just the same thing and there were very likely some who were telling the truth—that disillusionment, like all fashion, started in the upper strata of society and filtered through to the lower, which wear it out, and that nowadays those who are really bored most of all try to hide their misfortune like a vice. The staff captain did not understand these subtleties; he shook his head and smiled slyly:

"I suppose that it was the French who introduced this fashion of tedium?"

"No, the English!"

"Ah! So that's it!" he replied, "but then I suppose they always were thorough drunkards!"

I could not help thinking of a certain Moscow lady who insisted that Byron was nothing more than a drunkard. Actually, the staff captain's remark was more excusable: in order to refrain from wine, he naturally tried to convince himself that all misfortunes in the world derived from drunkenness.

Meanwhile, he continued his story in this way:

"Kazbich didn't appear again. But I don't know why I couldn't get the idea out of my head that he hadn't come down for nothing and that he was plotting something evil.

"Well, one day Pechorin talked me into going with him after wild boar. I withstood him for some time: after all, wild boar meant nothing to me. However, he dragged me off with him all the same. We took five soldiers with us and left early in the morning. We poked about the reeds and in the forest until ten o'clock—no animal. 'Hey, let's go back,' I said, 'Why be obstinate? Surely it's obvious that this isn't our lucky day.' But Grigory didn't want to return without a kill in spite of the heat and weariness. He was that sort of man: what he set his heart on he must have. Obviously as a child he had been his mother's spoiled little boy. At last, at noon, we sought out a damned boar—paff, paff—but it wasn't there anymore—got away into the reeds . . . it was that sort of unlucky day. So we rested a little and then headed for home.

"We were riding in line, silently, with reins slack and were almost up to the fort itself—only the scrub hid it from us—when suddenly there was a shot. We glanced at one another and were struck by the same thought. We galloped off straight toward the shot and saw that soldiers had gathered on the wall in a little crowd and were pointing to the plain. There was a rider flying headlong, holding something white over his saddle. Grigory screamed as well as any Chechen, snatched his musket from its case, and was off after him.

"Fortunately, since our hunt had been unsuccessful, our horses weren't tired; they tore off under us and every moment brought us nearer and nearer. At last I recognized Kazbich, but I couldn't make out what he was holding in front of him. I had caught up with Pechorin and called out to him, 'It's

Kazbich!' He looked around at me, nodded, and whipped up his horse.

"At last we were within rifle range of him; either Kazbich's horse was tired out or else worse than ours because, in spite of all his efforts, it wasn't going at any great pace. I think that at that moment he must have thought of his Karagyoz . . .

"I saw that Pechorin was taking aim with his rifle on the run. 'Don't shoot,' I shouted to him, 'Hold your fire; we'll run him down.' That's young blood for you. It always gets overheated at the wrong time. But the shot came, and the bullet pierced the horse's hind leg. Rashly, it ran on for another dozen paces, stumbled, and fell on to its knees. Kazbich jumped off it, and then we noticed that in his arms he was carrying a woman, wrapped up in a yashmak. It was Bela . . . poor Bela! He shouted something to us in his own language and held his dagger up over her. There was no point in delaying; I fired in my turn, at random; the bullet must have hit him in the shoulder, for he suddenly dropped his arm. . . . When the smoke cleared, the wounded horse was lying on the ground and beside it Bela; but Kazbich had thrown his musket away and was scrambling through the bushes and up a cliff, like a cat. I wanted to pick him off there but I didn't have a round ready. We jumped off our horses and rushed toward Bela. The poor thing, she lay motionless, and blood was flowing from the wound. What a villain he was! He might just as well have struck her in the heart and everything would have been over at once, but in the back . . . the most dastardly blow of all! She was unconscious. We tore off the yashmak and tied up the wound as tightly as we could; Pechorin kissed her cold lips without response—nothing could bring her around. Pechorin mounted his horse, I lifted her off the ground and somehow or other set her on his saddle; he put his arm around her and we rode back. After a few moments' silence Grigory said to me, 'Listen, Maxim, we won't get her back alive at this rate.' 'You're right,' I said—and we spurred the horses on to full speed. A crowd of people was waiting for us at the fort; carefully we carried the wounded girl to Pechorin's quarters and sent for the doctor. He was drunk, but he came all the same. He examined the wound and declared that she could not live more than a day. But he was wrong."

"She recovered?" I asked the staff captain, grasping his arm and rejoicing in spite of myself.

"No," he replied, "the doctor was wrong only insofar as she lived on for two more days."

"Tell me how Kazbich managed to kidnap her."

"Well, this is how: in spite of Pechorin's ban, she had gone out of the fort to the river. It was very hot, you know. She sat down on a boulder and lowered her feet into the water. Well, Kazbich sneaked up, grasped her, gagged her, and then dragged her off into the scrub. Then he jumped onto his horse and off he galloped. In the meantime she had managed to cry out, the sentries raised the alarm, shot and missed, and then we rushed up."

"Why did Kazbich want to take her away?"

"My dear fellow! These Circassians are well known as a nation of thieves: they can't help pinching anything that's left in their way; they don't need a reason, they just steal it . . . you can't blame them. Anyway he had liked the look of her for a long time."

"So Bela died?"

"She died; but she suffered for a long time and we suffered with her. She regained consciousness at about ten o'clock that evening. We were sitting at her bedside. As soon as she opened her eyes she began to call for Pechorin. 'I am here beside you,

my *djanechka* (that is, "darling," in our language),'
he answered taking her hand. 'I am going to die!'
she said. We began to soothe her, telling her that
the doctor had promised to cure her for certain;
she shook her little head and turned toward the wall;
she did not want to die.

"That night she became delirious: her head was
burning, and from time to time a feverish shudder
would pass through her body. She spoke wandering-
ly about her father, her brother; she wanted to be
in the mountains, at home. Afterward she spoke
about Pechorin too, calling him all sorts of tender
names or scolding him for falling out of love with
his *djanechka*.

"He listened to her in silence, resting his head on
his hands; but I didn't see a single tear on his eyelashes during the whole time. I don't know if he
couldn't cry or if he had control over his feelings.
As far as I was concerned, I never saw anything
sadder in my life.

"Toward morning the delirium passed. For an
hour she lay motionless and pale, and so weak that
it was hardly possible to see if she were breathing.
Later she improved and began to talk—only about
what, do you think? An idea like that only comes
to someone who is dying! She began to grieve because she was not a Christian, that her soul would
never meet Grigory's in the other world, and that
some other woman would be his companion in
paradise. I had the idea of baptizing her before
she died. I suggested this to her; she looked at me
irresolutely and didn't manage to say anything for
a long time; at last she replied that she would die in
the faith into which she had been born. So the
whole day passed. How she altered in that day!
The pale cheeks sank, the eyes grew bigger and

bigger, her lips burned. She felt the inner burning like a red-hot iron lying on her breast.

"Another night came. We didn't close an eye, didn't move from her bedside. She was suffering terribly, and groaning, but as soon as the pain began to abate she assured Grigory that she was better, tried to persuade him to go to bed, kissed his hand, didn't take her eyes off him. Toward dawn she began to feel the death pangs and started to thresh about, tearing off the bandages. The blood began to flow again. When we tied up the wound, she quieted down for a moment and asked Pechorin to kiss her. He knelt down beside the bed, lifted her head from the pillow, and pressed his lips to her cold lips. She wound her trembling arms tightly around his neck as if she wanted to give him her soul in this embrace. No, she did well to die. What would have become of her if Grigory had left her? And that would have happened sooner or later.

"For half the following day she was quiet, silent, and docile while our doctor tortured her with poultices and medicines. 'For goodness' sake!' I said to him, 'you said yourself that she's going to die in any case, so why all your preparations?' 'All the same, Maxim, it's better that one's conscience should be easy!' he replied. A good conscience indeed!

"In the afternoon she became terribly thirsty. We opened the window, but it was hotter outside than in the room; we put ice by the bed, but nothing helped. I knew that this unbearable thirst was a sign that the end was approaching, and I told Pechorin so. 'Water, water,' she was saying in a hoarse voice, raising herself on the bed.

"He turned as white as a sheet, grabbed a glass, filled it, and gave it to her. I covered my eyes with my hands and began to recite a prayer, I don't remember which one it was. Yes, my dear fellow, I have seen many people die in the hospitals and on the battlefield, but not like that, not at all like that. . . . I must confess that it still saddens me to think that she didn't once remember me before she died, and you know, I loved her like a father. Well, God will forgive her! But after all, who am I that people should think of me before they die?

"As soon as she had drunk the water she became easier and within three minutes she died. We put a mirror to her lips. It was clear! I took Pechorin out of the room, and we went to the fort wall; for a long time we walked up and down together in silence, our hands clasped behind our backs; his face didn't show any particular emotion, and I became annoyed; if I had been in his place, I would have died of grief. Eventually he sat down on the ground in the shade and began to draw something in the sand with his stick. You know, I wanted to console him for decency's sake and I began to talk. He lifted his head and burst out laughing. That laugh made my flesh creep. I went to make arrangements about the coffin.

"I suppose I occupied myself with this partly for diversion. I had a piece of Persian cloth and covered the coffin with it and decorated it with some Caucasian silver lace which Grigory had bought for her.

"We buried her early the next morning outside the fort near the spot where she had sat for the last time. White acacia and elder bushes have grown around her grave now. I would have liked to have placed a cross but, you understand, it wasn't quite right—after all she wasn't a Christian . . ."

"And what of Pechorin?" I asked.

"Pechorin wasn't well for a long time—became quite emaciated, poor soul. But from that time we never spoke about Bela; I saw that it would be unpleasant for him, so what point was there? Three months later he was posted to the Y——ski regiment, and he left for Georgia. I haven't seen him since. But I do recall that recently someone was telling me that he had returned to Russia, but it wasn't in corps orders. But then a near one is always the last to hear."

Here he entered on a long dissertation on how unpleasant it is to hear news a year later—very likely to stifle his unhappy memories.

I did not interrupt him, nor did I listen.

After an hour the opportunity came to leave. The snowstorm had abated, the sky cleared, and we set off. On the road I could not help leading the conversation around to Bela and Pechorin again.

"Did you ever hear what happened to Kazbich?" I enquired.

"Kazbich? I really don't know. I did hear that there is some Kazbich on the Shapsug right flank, a daring fellow who rides about slowly in a red cloak in the midst of our fire and bows very politely when a bullet passes close by. But it can hardly be the same man."

Maxim and I parted at Kobi. I went on with post-horses, but he could not follow me on account of his heavy baggage. We did not expect ever to meet again, but we did, and if you like, I will tell you about it: it is a story in itself. Will you admit, though, that Maxim is a man who deserves respect? If you do admit this, I shall be fully rewarded for my story, which has perhaps been overly long.

Maxim Maximich

Having parted from Maxim I galloped briskly through the Terek and Daryal passes, lunched in Kazbek, had tea in Lars, and reached Vladikavkaz in time for supper. I shall spare you from descriptions of the mountains, from exclamations which convey nothing, from pictures which depict nothing, particularly to those who have not been there, and from statistical observations, which, certainly, no one will read.

I stopped at an inn where all travelers stay and where, at the time, there was no one to roast a pheasant or make some soup since the three invalids to whom the place had been entrusted were either idiots or so drunk that one could not get any sense out of them.

They told me that I must stay there for three days since the "event" had not yet arrived from Ekaterinograd and consequently one could not start back. What an "event"! . . . But a bad pun is no consolation to a Russian and to amuse myself in the meanwhile I decided to write down Maxim's story about Bela, not imagining that it would be the first link in a long chain of stories. You see how a trivial incident can sometimes have cruel consequences! . . . But perhaps you do not know what an "event" is?

It is an escort consisting of an infantry platoon and guns which accompanies the baggage trains across the Kabard from Vladikavkaz to Ekaterinograd.*

I was very bored the first day. Early the next morning a carriage drove into the yard. "Well! Maxim Maximich!" We greeted each other like old friends. I offered him my room. He did not stand on ceremony, he even thumped me on the shoulder and twisted his mouth by way of a smile. What a quaint fellow he was!

Maxim possessed a knowledge of the culinary art which was profound. He roasted a pheasant amazingly well and smothered it successfully with cucumber pickle. I must admit that without him I would have been on very short rations. A bottle of Kakhetin helped us forget the meager choice of dishes which were all alike, and, lighting our pipes, we sat down—I, by the window, he, by the over-filled stove, because the day was damp and cold. We said nothing. What had we to talk about? He had already told me everything interesting about himself and I had nothing to tell. I looked out of the window. A number of mean little houses scattered along the bank of the Terek, which flowed broader and broader, were visible from time to time behind the trees, and farther away, a jagged wall of mountains showed dark blue and the Kazbek looked out from behind in its white cardinal's miter. I bade them farewell in my thoughts: I was sorry to leave them.

We sat like this for a long time. The sun had hidden itself behind the cold peaks, and a whitish mist had begun to spread over the valleys, when from the street there came the ringing of a carriage bell and the shouting of drivers. Several car-

riages with some grubby Armenians drove into the
yard of the inn followed by an empty long-distance
carriage whose easy movement, practical construction, and luxurious appearance had a certain foreign
stamp. Behind it walked a man with large mous-
tachios, in a Hungarian cap, quite well-dressed for
a valet; one could not mistake his calling because of the dashing way he shook the ashes out
of his pipe and shouted at the drivers. He was
obviously the spoiled servant of a lazy master—a
sort of Russian Figaro.

"Tell me, my man," I shouted to him through the
window, "what is this—has the "event" arrived?"

He looked over rather insolently, straightened his
cravat, and turned away. The Armenian walking
next to him smiled and answered for him that the
"event" had indeed arrived and would turn back the
next morning.

"Thank God," said Maxim, walking up to the
window at that moment. "What a marvelous carriage!" he added, "some official must be going to
Tiflis on an inquiry. He obviously doesn't know our
mountains! They're not for the likes of you, old
fellow; they'll shake even an English carriage to
pieces!"

"But let's go and find out who it really is."

We went out into the corridor. At the end of it
a door to a side room was open. The valet and the
driver were dragging trunks into it.

"Listen, my lad," the staff captain asked him,
"whose is that marvelous carriage? Eh? It's a
beautiful carriage." The valet did not turn around
but muttered something to himself as he untied a
trunk. Maxim became annoyed; he touched the
uncivil fellow on the shoulder and said, "I am
talking to you, my man."

"Whose carriage? My master's."

"And who is your master?"

"Pechorin."

"What's that? What did you say? Pechorin? Well, goodness me! Didn't he serve in the Caucasus?" Maxim exclaimed, tugging at my sleeve. Joy shone in his eyes.

"I think he did—but I haven't been with him long."

"Well! . . . Quite so! . . . Grigory Alexandrovich? . . . Is that his name? I was a friend of your master's," he added, giving the valet's shoulder a friendly thump that made him stagger.

"Pardon me, sir, you are interfering with me," he said, scowling.

"Don't be foolish, my man! Don't you understand that your master and I were intimate friends, lived together . . . Where is he staying?" The servant informed us that Pechorin had stopped at Colonel N.'s for supper and the night.

"Won't he call in here this evening?" said Maxim, "or perhaps you will go to him for something? If you do, tell him that Maxim Maximich is here; and tell him . . .he will know . . . I will give you eight silver kopeks for vodka . . ."

The valet turned up his nose on hearing such a mean offer, but assured Maxim that he would carry out his mission.

"He's bound to come running over here straightaway!" Maxim told me with a look of triumph, "I'll go outside the gates and wait for him. . . . Oh dear! It's a pity I don't know N. . . ."

Maxim sat down on a bench outside the gates, and I went away to my room. I admit that I waited for the appearance of this Pechorin with impatience too; although I had not formed a very good opinion of him from the staff captain's story, nevertheless there were certain features in his character which seemed to me to be remarkable. An hour later one of the invalids brought in a boiling samovar and a teapot.

"Maxim, don't you want some tea?" I called to him through the window.

"Thank you very much. I don't want any."

"Oh, drink some! It's getting late and it's cold."

"It doesn't matter. Thank you very much."

"Well, as you like." I began to have tea by myself; ten minutes later the old man came in:

"I suppose you're right. I'd better have a cup— I've been waiting all the time. . . . The man went to him a long time ago, but something must have detained him."

He drank up his cup hurriedly, refused a second, and with a certain restlessness went outside the gates again; it was clear that Pechorin's neglect distressed the old man, the more so since he had recently been talking to me about his friendship with him and only an hour before had been certain that he would run across as soon as he heard his name. It was already dark and late when I opened the window again and began to call Maxim, saying that it was time to go to bed; he muttered something between clenched teeth; I repeated the invitation—he did not reply. I wrapped myself up in my cloak and lay down on the divan; I dozed off quickly and would have slept through peacefully if, when it was already very late, Maxim had not come into the room and disturbed me. He threw his pipe onto the table and began to walk about the room. He poked the stove and at last lay down, but coughed, spat, and tossed about for a long while.

"Are the bugs biting you?" I asked.

"Yes, the bugs . . ." he replied, sighing heavily.

I woke up early the next morning; but Maxim had preceded me. I found him by the gates sitting on a bench. "I must call on the commandant," he said, "so if Pechorin should come, would you please send for me? . . ." I promised to do so. He ran off as if his limbs had acquired a youthful strength and suppleness again.

It was a fresh but fine morning. Golden clouds towered above the mountains like another range of heavenly mountains; there was a broad square in front of the gates; beyond it the bazaar was crowded with people because it was Sunday; barefooted Osset boys shouldering bundles filled with honeycombs over their shoulders circled around me; I chased them away. I was not in the mood for them: I had begun to share the good staff captain's disquiet.

Ten minutes had not passed when the man we were waiting for appeared at the end of the square. He was walking with Colonel N., who conducted him to the inn, said good-bye to him, and turned off toward the fort. I sent one of the invalids for Maxim immediately.

The valet came out to meet Pechorin and reported that the horses would be harnessed right away, gave him a box of cigars, and, receiving several instructions, went away to get busy. His master lit a cigar, yawned twice, and sat down on a bench on the far side of the gates. Now I ought to draw his portrait for you.

He was of average height; his well-shaped, slender figure and broad shoulders indicated a strong physique capable of enduring all the hardships of a wandering life and changes of climate. It was untouched by the debauchery of metropolitan life or by inner storms. His dusty velvet frock coat was fastened only by the two lower buttons, allowing one to see his blindingly white linen, which indicated the habits of a respectable man. His soiled gloves seemed especially made for his small, aristocratic hands, and when he took off one glove, I was surprised by the thinness of his pale fingers. His walk was careless and lazy, but I noticed that he did not wave his arms about—a sure sign of a certain reticence of character. By the way, these are my personal remarks, based on my own observations, and I do not want to make you believe in them blindly. When he sat down on the bench, his upright figure bent over as if there were not a single bone in his spine. The position of his entire body reflected some sort of nervous weakness. He sat like one of Balzac's thirty-year-old coquettes on her down-upholstered armchair after a tiring ball. From the first look at his face I would not have thought him more than twenty-three, though later I was ready to credit him with thirty. There was something childlike in his smile. His skin had a certain feminine softness. His pale, noble forehead was edged very prettily with blond, naturally curly hair, and on it one could detect only after long observation the marks of wrinkles which crossed each other and probably stood out much more clearly in moments of anger or mental stress. In spite of the light color of his hair, his moustache and eyebrows were black—a sign of breeding in a man just as a black mane and a black tail are on a white horse. To complete this portait I will say that he had a slightly turned-up nose, dazzling white teeth, and hazel eyes—I ought to say a few more words about the eyes.

In the first place, they did not laugh when he laughed. Have you never noticed an oddity like this in certain people? It is a sign either of an evil temper or else of constant melancholy. From behind his partly lowered eyelashes they shone with a certain phosphorescent brilliance, if one can so express it. It was not the reflection of sincere warmth or of a darting imagination: it was a brilliance like the brilliance of smooth steel, blinding, but cold. His glance, though it did not last long, was piercing and heavy and left one with the unpleasant impression of an indiscreet question; it might have seemed insolent, if it were not so indifferently calm. Perhaps all these remarks came into my mind only because I knew certain details of his life, and perhaps upon someone else he would have made a completely different impression. In conclusion I will say that he was on the whole very good-looking and possessed one of those singular physiognomies which are particularly pleasing to women.

The horses were already harnessed; from time to time the small bell under the arch rang out, and the valet had already gone up to Pechorin twice with the report that everything was ready, but Maxim had still not appeared. Fortunately, Pechorin was immersed in thought, looking at the dark blue teeth of the Caucasus, and was apparently in no hurry for the road. I went up to him.

"If you care to wait a little longer," I said, "you will have the pleasure of seeing an old friend."

"Oh, that's right," he answered quickly, "they told me yesterday; but where is he?" I turned toward the square and caught sight of Maxim running with all his might. In a few moments he was beside us; he could hardly breathe; sweat was streaming down his face; wet tufts of gray hair poked out from under his cap and stuck to his forehead; his knees were shaking. He wanted to throw himself around Pechorin's neck, but the latter, quite coldly, though with an affable smile, stretched out a hand toward him. The staff captain was stupefied for a moment, but then grasped his hand greedily with both of his: he still could not speak.

"How glad I am, Maxim Maximich! Well, how are you getting on?" said Pechorin.

"And . . . thou? And you?" the old man muttered
with tears in his eyes, uncertain whether to use the
second person familiar or formal and deciding on
the latter, "how many years . . . how many days it's
been . . . where are you off to?"

"I am going to Persia—and beyond."

"Not this moment surely? Wait a bit, my dearest
fellow! Surely we're not going to part this minute?
We haven't seen each other for such a long time . . ."

"It's time for me to go, Maxim Maximich," was
the answer.

"Goodness me, goodness me! Why are you leaving in such a hurry? I had so much to say to you
. . . so many questions to ask . . . Well, why? Are
you going into exile? . . . What? . . . what have you
been up to?"

"I was bored!" replied Pechorin with a smile.

"Do you remember the life we led in the fort?
Marvelous country for hunting. You know you were
a passionate lover of shooting . . . And Bela?"

Pechorin paled very slightly and turned away.

"Yes, I remember," he said, and almost immediately he had to yawn. Maxim started to talk him
into staying with him two hours longer.

"We'll have a first-rate dinner," he was saying,
"I've got two pheasants, and the Kakhetin here is
marvelous—not like the stuff in Georgia, of course,
but the best quality. We'll have a chat . . . you will
tell me about your life in St. Petersburg . . . Eh?"

"Really, I have nothing to tell, dear Maxim Maximich. But farewell, it's time for me to go. I'm in a
hurry . . . Thank you for not forgetting . . ." he
added, taking him by the hand.

The old man knitted his brows. He was sad and
annoyed although he tried to hide it.

"Forget!" he growled, "I have forgotten nothing.

. . . Well, God be with you! I didn't imagine meeting you like this . . ."

"That's enough, that's enough," said Pechorin,
giving him a friendly embrace, "am I really not the
same? What can one do? Each to his own road.
God knows if we'll ever meet again! . . ." Saying
this he was already sitting down in the carriage, and
the driver had started to gather up the reins.

"Wait, wait!" Maxim called out suddenly, seizing
the doors of the carriage, "I nearly forgot all about
it. . . . I've still got your papers, Grigory Alexandrovich. I cart them about with me. I thought I'd find
you in Georgia, but here is where God would have
us meet. . . . What shall I do with them?"

"Whatever you like!" replied Pechorin. "Farewell . . ."

"So you're off to Persia? When are you coming
back?" Maxim called after him.

The carriage was already some way off. Yet
Pechorin made a sign with his hand, which could
have been interpreted in the following way: It's
uncertain . . . there's no point anyway.

The sound of the bell and the rumble of wheels
on the flinty road had long passed out of hearing,
but the poor old man was still standing on the
same spot, deep in thought.

"Yes," he said at last, trying to adopt a disin-
terested look although tears of chagrin shone on his
eyelashes at times, "of course we were friends—well,
what are friends these days? . . . What am I to him?
I am not rich, I don't hold high rank, and I'm certainly not his equal in years. . . . Look what a dandy
he's become now he's been in St. Petersburg again.
What a carriage . . . so much luggage . . . and such
a proud valet . . ." These words were pronounced
with an ironic smile.

"Tell me," he continued, turning toward me,

"what do you think of it? Well, what demon's carrying him off to Persia now? It's funny, my God, it's funny! You know I always knew he was a light-minded fellow on whom one couldn't rely. But, really, I'm sorry that he's going to come to a bad end . . . indeed it can't be otherwise! I always said that there's no use for anyone who forgets his old friends! . . ." Here he turned away in order to hide his emotion and went off to walk about the courtyard by his carriage, pretending he was inspecting the wheels when his eyes, as they did every moment, filled with tears.

"Maxim," I said, going up to him, "what are the papers Pechorin left with you?"

"God knows. Some sort of journal."

"What are you going to do with them?"

"What? I'll have cartridges made of them."

"Give them over to me, rather."

He looked at me with surprise, muttered something between clenched teeth, and started to rummage in his trunk; then he pulled out a notebook and threw it contemptuously onto the ground; then another, a third, and a tenth received the same treatment; there was something childish in his spite; I felt amused and sorry.

"There they all are," he said. "I congratulate you on your find."

"And I may do anything I like with them?"

"You can print them in the papers if you like. What's it got to do with me? Am I some friend or relation of his? True, we lived for a long time under the same roof . . . But then I have lived with any number of people."

I snatched up the papers and took them away quickly, fearing that the staff captain might change his mind. Soon they came and announced to us that the "event" would move in an hour: I bade them pack. I was already putting on my cap when the staff captain came into the room; he did not seem to be preparing to leave; he had a certain strained, cold look.

"Aren't you going, Maxim?"

"No, sir."

"Why not?"

"I still haven't seen the commandant and I've got certain official business to attend to."

"But haven't you already been to see him?"

"Of course I've been," he said, busying himself, "but he wasn't in . . . and I didn't wait for him."

I understood: for the first time in his life, perhaps, the poor old man had abandoned service affairs for a private matter, to use official language, and, indeed, how he had been rewarded!

"I'm sorry," I told him, "very sorry that we've got to part so soon."

"How can we uneducated old men keep up with you? You young society people are proud: for a time you're in the midst of Circassian bullets, then you go off here or there, and afterward when you meet you're even ashamed to stretch out a hand to the likes of me."

"I haven't deserved these reproaches, Maxim."

"I'm only talking by the way, you know; however, I wish you every happiness and a good journey."

We said good-bye rather dryly. The good Maxim Maximich had become an obstinate, cantankerous staff captain. And why? Because Pechorin, through absentmindedness or for some other reason, had stretched out his hand to him when he wanted him to fall on his neck! It is sad to see a young man lose his finest hopes and dreams when the rose-colored glasses through which he has looked at human affairs and feelings are torn from him. Nevertheless there is the hope he will replace his old delusions with new ones no less transient but, on the other hand, no less sweet. But what can one replace them with at Maxim's age? The heart must harden and the spirit close up.

I departed alone.

Pechorin's Journal

Author's Note

I heard recently that Pechorin had died on his return from Persia. This news made me very glad; it gave me the right to publish these memoirs, and I have taken the opportunity of putting my name to a stranger's work. May God prevent readers from punishing me for such an innocent deception.

Now I ought to explain some of the reasons which led me to place before the public the innermost secrets of a man I never knew. Well might I still be his friend: everyone understands the crafty indiscretions of a real friend; but I only saw him once in my life on the high road; consequently I cannot harbor that unspeakable hatred toward him which is hidden under the cover of friendship and waits only for the death of the loved one, or his misfortune, to bring down upon his head a hail of reproaches, advice, derision, and pity.

While reading these memoirs I became convinced of the innocence of the man who brought his own weaknesses and vices so mercilessly to light. The story of a human soul, even the smallest of souls, is hardly less interesting and useful than the history of a whole nation, especially when it is the result of self-examination on the part of a mature mind and written without any vain desire to arouse sympathy or surprise. Rousseau's *Confessions* has this very failing, in that he read them to his friends.

And so it was only the wish to be of some good that induced me to publish extracts from a journal which came into my hands by chance. Although I have changed all proper names, those who are mentioned in it will no doubt recognize themselves, and perhaps they will find some justification for those deeds for which they have blamed the man, who henceforth will have nothing in common with this world: we almost always forgive what we understand.

I have included in this book only that which relates to Pechorin's stay in the Caucasus; I still have a thick notebook in which he tells the story of his whole life. Some day this too will be submitted to the judgment of the world; but at the moment I cannot take this responsibility on myself for many important reasons.

Perhaps some readers would like to know my opinion of Pechorin's character. My answer is the title of this book. "But that's a wicked irony!" they will say. I do not know.

Taman

Taman is the nastiest little seaboard town in Russia. Not only did I very nearly die of hunger there, but on top of that they wanted to drown me. I arrived late at night on a post wagon. The coachman stopped the tired troika by the gates of the only stone house, at the entrance to the town. The sentry, a Black Sea Cossack, half-awake, cried out wildly, "Who's there?" when he heard the little bell ringing. A sergeant and a lance corporal came out. I explained that I was an officer going to an active unit on official business, and demanded government quarters. The lance corporal took us around the town. Every hut we drove up to was occupied. It was cold, I had not slept for three nights, I was tired out and began to get angry. "Take me somewhere, you robber, to the devil if you like, but get me some sort of place," I cried. "There is one other dwelling," replied the lance corporal, scratching the back of his neck, "but your highness won't like it; it's a bad place." I did not appreciate the exact meaning of the last remark and ordered him to proceed. After much wandering through dirty alleyways, where I saw only dilapidated fences along the sides, we drove up to a small peasant's hut on the very shore of the sea.

A full moon was shining on the reed roof and white walls of my new home; in the courtyard, which was enclosed by a cobbled wall, stood another crooked little hovel, smaller and more ancient than the first. A steep bank led down to the sea almost from its very walls, and below, the dark-blue waves were splashing with a continual murmur. The moon looked calmly on her restless but obedient element, the sea, and by her light I could make out two boats, far from the shore, their black rigging etched on the pale horizon like spiders' webs. "There are ships in the harbor," I thought, "I shall leave for Gelendzhik tomorrow." A Cossack of the line was assigned to me as an orderly. I bade him unload my truck and dismiss the driver, and began to call out for the master of the house—silence. I banged—silence. What was this? At last a boy of fourteen crept out of the shadows. "Where's the master?" "No here." "What? Not here at all?" "Not at all." "And the mistress?" "Gone away to the village." "Who's going to open the door for me?" I said, kicking it. The door opened by itself; a musty smell drifted out of the hut. I struck a sulfur match and lifted it to the boy's nose: I saw by its light two white eyes. He was blind, completely blind from birth. He stood stock-still in front of me, and I began to examine the features of his face.

I must admit that I am strongly prejudiced against all those who are blind, crooked, deaf, dumb, legless, armless, hunchbacked, and the like. I have remarked that there is invariably some kind of strange connection between the outward appearance of a person and his soul—as if with the loss of a limb, the soul lost some feeling or other.

And so I began to study the blind boy's face; but what can one read in a face which has no eyes? I had been looking at him with unwilling pity for a long time when, suddenly, a barely noticeable smile ran across his thin lips, and I do not know why, but it gave me a most unpleasant impression. A suspicion arose in my mind that this blind boy was not as blind as he appeared; in vain I tried to convince myself that it was impossible to fake walleye —and what point was there in doing it even if one could? But what was I to do? I am often inclined to prejudice.

"You're the master's son?" I asked him at last. "No." "Who are you then?" "Orphan, beggar." "Has the mistress any children?" "No; there was daughter but she ran off to sea with a Tatar." "With which Tatar?" "Devil knows! Crimean Tatar, boatman from Kerch."

I went inside the hut: two benches and a table and an immense chest by the stove made up the entire furniture. There was not a single icon on the wall—a bad sign! The sea wind was blowing through a broken window. I pulled a wax candle-end out of the trunk, lit it, and began to unpack my things. I put my saber and musket in the corner, laid my pistols on the table, spread my felt cloak over one bench. My Cossack stretched out on the other. Within ten minutes he had begun to snore, but I could not sleep: the boy with white eyes was moving in front of me in the gloom.

Thus an hour passed. The moon shone through the window and its beam played on the earthen floor of the hut. Suddenly a shadow fell across the bright strip that bisected the floor. I raised myself a little and looked out of the window: again someone ran past it and disappeared God knows where. I could not believe that this creature had run down the perpendicular bank, but there was nowhere else it could have gone. I got up, put on my coat, belted on my dagger, and went out of the hut very quietly; the blind boy was coming toward me. I flattened myself against the wall and held my breath; he went past me with a sure but careful step. Under his arm he was carrying some sort of bundle. He turned toward the boat landing and began to go down a narrow, twisting path. "On that day the dumb will sing out and the blind will see," I thought, following him at some distance but close enough not to lose sight of him.

Meanwhile, the moon was being hidden by clouds and a mist had risen on the sea; the lantern on the stern of a nearby boat hardly shone through it. Close to the shore there gleamed the foam of the breaking waves, which threatened to engulf the boat at any moment. I went down, negotiating the steep hill with difficulty, and then I saw the blind boy halt and turn away, down to the right. He was walking so close to the water that it seemed a wave would catch him at any moment and carry him away; but obviously this was not his first walk, to judge by the assurance with which he stepped from stone to stone and avoided the gaps in between. At last he stopped, as if listening for something; he sat on the ground and put the bundle down beside him. I watched his movements from behind a rock which overhung the shore. A few minutes later a white figure appeared from the opposite side; it ran up to the blind boy and sat down beside him. From time to time the wind carried their conversation up to me.

"What do you think, blind one?" said a woman's voice. "The gale is fierce; Yanko won't come."

"Yanko isn't afraid of gales," he answered.

"This mist is getting thicker," the woman's voice retorted, sadly.

"It's easier to get past the patrol boats in a mist," was the answer.

"But if he gets drowned?"

"Well, what of that? You'll go to church on Sunday without a new ribbon."

A silence followed. But one thing amazed me: the blind boy had spoken to me in Ukrainian dialect, but now he was expressing himself in pure Russian.

"You see I'm right," the blind boy spoke again, clapping his hands. "Yanko isn't afraid of the sea, or the winds, or the mist, or the coast patrols. Listen: that isn't water splashing, it doesn't deceive me—it's the splashing of long oars."

The woman jumped up and began to peer into the distance, agitatedly.

"You're delirious, blind one," she said, "I don't see anything."

I must confess that however hard I tried to make out something like a boat in the distance, I had no success. Thus ten minutes passed; then a black dot appeared out there among the mountainous waves; it grew larger and then smaller again. Rising slowly on the crests of the waves and swiftly sliding down them, a boat was drawing near to the shore. It was a daring oarsman who decided to cross the strait at a distance of more than thirteen miles on a night like that, and the reason that impelled him must have been important indeed. Thinking these thoughts, I looked at the poor boat with an involuntary quickening of the heart. But it plunged like a duck, and then, beating its oars quickly like wings, it leaped out of the abyss through splashes of foam. I thought it would crash against the shore and break into pieces, but it turned side-on adroitly and sped safely into a little cove. A man of medium height in a Tatar sheepskin cap jumped ashore; he waved his hand, and all three set about pulling something out of the boat; the load was so heavy that to this day I cannot understand why it hadn't sunk the boat. Each shouldering a bundle they set out along the shore, and I soon lost sight of them. I had to return to my lodgings; but I admit that all these strange events had alarmed me, and I waited for the morning with impatience.

My Cossack was very surprised when he woke up to see me fully dressed; I did not tell him the reason, however. Having feasted my eyes for a short while on the blue sky, strewn with shreds of clouds and on the distant shore of the Crimea, a lilac-colored strip ending in a cliff at whose summit a tower looms white, I set off to the fort of Fanagoria to find out from the commandant about the time of my departure from Gelendzhik.

But alas, the commandant could give me no definite indication. The vessels at the landing stage were all either patrol boats or merchantmen which had not yet even started to load. "Perhaps the packet boat will arrive in three or four days' time," said the commandant, "and then we'll see." I returned home sullen and angry. My Cossack met me at the door with a frightened face.

"Looks bad, your honor," he said to me.

"Yes, brother, God knows when we'll leave here." He grew even more alarmed, and bending over toward me, said in a whisper: "It's evil here! I met a Black Sea sergeant today, I know him—he was in our detachment last year; when I told him where we were staying he told me: 'It's evil here, brother, the people are bad!' And really what sort of blind fellow is that one? Goes everywhere alone, to the bazaar, for bread, for water . . . it's obvious they're all used to it here."

"What of it? Has the mistress appeared at last?"

"An old woman and her daughter came today when you were away."

"What daughter? She hasn't got a daughter."

"God knows who she is if she isn't her daughter,

but the old woman's over there now in her own hut."

I went into the hovel. The stove was burning fiercely and a dinner was cooking in it—quite a rich dinner for poor people. To all my questions the old woman replied that she was deaf and could not hear. What could one do with her? I turned to the blind boy who was sitting in front of the stove putting brushwood on the fire. "Well, you blind little devil," I said, taking him by the ear, "tell me, where were you going to with the bundle last night, eh?" Suddenly, my blind boy burst into tears, cried out, moaned, "Where'd I go? Nowhere. And I don't know about any bundle." The old woman heard this time and began muttering, "So that's what you think, and of a poor wretch too! What do you want with him? What's he done to you?" I found this tedious and went outside, firmly resolved to find an answer to this riddle.

I wrapped myself up in my cloak, sat down on a stone by the wall, and looked into the distance. Before me stretched the sea, disturbed by last night's gale, and its monotonous noise, like the murmur of a crowded town, reminded me of years past, carried my thoughts to the north, to our cold metropolis. Disturbed by these recollections I forgot myself. Thus an hour passed, more perhaps. . . . Suddenly my ears caught something like a song. In fact it was a song sung by a fresh little female voice—but where was it coming from—I listened hard—it was a strange melody, now drawn-out and sad, now quick and lively. I looked around, but no one was about; I listened hard again: the sounds seemed to come from the sky. I raised my eyes: a girl in a striped dress, with loose tresses, a real mermaid, was standing on the roof of my hut. Shading her eyes from the rays of the sun with her hand, she was looking

fixedly into the distance. Sometimes she laughed and
argued with herself, sometimes she sang the song
again.

I remember that song word for word:

> *As by free will they are driven*
> *Crossing the green seas*
> *All the little ships are sailing*
> *With their white sails hoisted.*
>
> *In the middle of this fleet*
> *Sails my little boat*
> *Little boat which has no rigging*
> *Carrying two oars.*
>
> *If a storm should threaten now*
> *Old and knowing mariners*
> *Will haul up the little wings*
> *And a path cut through the sea.*
>
> *To the sea I'll pray a prayer*
> *And bow down low;*
> *"Do not drown my little boatman*
> *Spare him, wicked sea:*
>
> *"Brings my little waterman*
> *Valuable goods and wares,*
> *Wares my reckless boatman steers*
> *Through the dark and stormy night."*

It came to me that I had heard the very same
voice the night before; I was lost in thought for a
minute and when I glanced at the roof again, the
girl was not there. Suddenly she whipped past me
singing something else, then, snapping her fingers,
ran in to the old woman and started an argument
with her. The old woman was angry, but the girl

was laughing loudly. Then I saw my mermaid skipping along again; coming past me she stopped and looked me fixedly in the eye as if surprised at my presence, after which she turned away carelessly and disappeared from the boat landing. It did not finish there. She stayed around my quarters the whole day; the singing and dancing did not stop for a minute. What an extraordinary creature! There were no signs of madness on her face; on the contrary, her eyes would rest on me with a shrewd penetration and seemed endowed with some sort of magnetic power. And all the time these eyes seemed to expect a question. But every time I started to speak she would run away with a cunning smile.

Certainly I had never seen a woman like that one. She was far from being a beauty, but then I have my prejudices about beauty, too. There was plenty of breeding in her, and breeding in women, as in horses, is an important thing; we owe this discovery to "Young France." It (that is, the breeding, not "Young France") is in the main revealed in bearing, in the arms and legs; the nose especially is of great significance. In Russia a straight nose is even rarer than a small foot. My songstress seemed no more than eighteen. Her unusually supple waist, the singular inclination of the head, which was quite natural to her, the long auburn hair, the golden tinge of the slightly sunburned skin on her neck and shoulders, and especially her straight nose —I found all of it bewitching. Although I read something wild and suspicious into her oblique glances, and although there was something uncertain in her smile, such are the powers of prejudice that the straight nose sent me out of my mind: I imagined I had found Goethe's Mignon, that quaint creation of his Germanic fantasy—and really there were many similarities between them: the same swift transitions from tremendous restlessness to complete immobility, the same enigmatic speeches, the same jumps and strange songs.

Stopping her by the door toward evening I had the following conversation with her:

"Tell me, my beauty," I asked, "what were you doing today on the roof?" "I was watching where the wind was blowing from." "How does that affect you?" "Whence the wind comes, thence comes happiness too." "Really? Perhaps you were summoning happiness by singing?" "Where there is singing, there too is rejoicing." "But what if you are singing yourself sorrow instead?" "Well, what of it? When things won't be better, they will be worse, and anyway from evil to good there is no great distance." "Who taught you that song?" "No one taught me; it comes into my head and I sing it; he who listens will hear, but he who ought not to hear will not understand." "What is your name, my songstress?" "He knows who christened me!" "But who christened you?" "I know who." "What a secretive girl you are! But I have found out something about you." (Her face did not change, she did not move her lips, as if it meant nothing to her.) "I have learned that you were walking on the shore last night." And then, very importantly, I told her everything that I saw, thinking it would disturb her—but not at all. She started to roar with laugher. "You saw much and know little, but keep what you do know locked up." "But suppose I had the idea of informing the commandant?" And here I adopted a very serious, even strict attitude. She suddenly jumped up, burst into song, and disappeared, like a little bird scared out of a bush. My last words were quite out of place; I did not suspect their significance at the time, but later I had occasion to regret them.

As soon as it got dark I ordered my Cossack to

warm the teapot, bivouac-style, lit a candle, and sat down at the table puffing at a little traveling pipe. I was just finishing my second glass of tea when suddenly the door creaked and I heard steps and the light rustling of a dress behind me; I started and turned round—it was she, my mermaid. She sat down quietly opposite me, without a word, and turned her eyes on mine, and I do not know why, but that gaze seemed peculiarly tender to me. It reminded me of one of those looks that used to sway my life in the old times. It seemed as if she were expecting a question, but I was silent, full of unutterable embarrassment. Her face was covered with a dull paleness that spoke of an inner emotion; her hand wandered aimlessly over the table, and I noticed it shaking slightly; her breasts were thrust out so high that it looked as if she were holding her breath. This comedy began to bore me and I was ready to interrupt the silence in the most prosaic way, that is by offering her a glass of tea, when suddenly she jumped up, wound her arms around my neck, and planted a moist, fervent kiss on my lips. My eyes went dim, my head spun, I clasped her in my arms with all the force of youthful passion, but she slipped through them like a snake, whispering in my ear: "Tonight, when everyone is asleep, come to the shore," and sped out of the room like an arrow. In the shadows, she upset the teapot and the candle which was standing on the floor. "What a she-devil!" cried the Cossack who was stretched out on the straw and thinking about warming up the remains of the tea. Only then did I collect myself.

Two hours later, when everything was quiet in the harbor, I roused my Cossack. "If I should fire my pistol," I told him, "run down to the shore." He rolled his eyes and answered automatically, "Yes, your highness." I stuck a pistol in my belt and went

out. She was waiting for me at the edge of the slope;
her clothing was more than scanty, a narrow shawl
girded her slender waist.

"Follow me!" she said taking me by the hand, and
we started to go down. I cannot understand how I
did not break my neck; below we turned to the
right and followed the same route along which I
had followed the blind boy the night before. The
moon had not yet risen and only two little stars, like
two warning beacons, sparkled on the dim blue
vault of the sky. Sluggish waves rolled slowly and
evenly one behind the other, scarcely lifting the only
boat that was moored to the shore. "Let's get into
the boat," said my companion. I hesitated—I am no
lover of sentimental trips on the sea—but I had no
time to beat a retreat. She jumped into the boat
with me behind her, and I had not yet managed to
collect myself when I noticed that we were afloat.
"What does this mean?" I said angrily. "It means,"
she answered, sitting me down on the thwart and
putting her arms around my waist, "it means that I
love you . . ." Her cheek pressed against mine, and
I felt her hot breath on my face. Suddenly, something fell noisily into the water: I clutched at my
belt—the pistol was gone. Ah, then an awful suspicion came over me, and the blood rushed to my
head. I looked out—we were about a hundred and
twenty yards from shore, and I do not know how to
swim! I wanted to push her away from me—she
clutched at my clothes like a cat, and suddenly a
powerful jolt very nearly threw me into the sea. The
boat started to roll, but I righted myself and a
desperate struggle ensued between us; despair gave
me strength, but I soon noticed that my opponent
was more agile than I. "What do you want?" I cried
out, taking a powerful grip on her small hands. Her

fingers creaked in the joints but she did not cry out: her snakelike nature withstood this torture.

"You saw," she answered, "you will report!" And with a superhuman effort she threw me down onto the gunwale. We both were hanging down from the boat, bending from the waist: her hair was touching the water. The moment was decisive. I rested my knee on the bottom of the boat, grasped her hair with one hand and her throat with the other. She let go of my clothing and in a flash I had thrown her down into the waves.

It was already quite dark; her head showed up twice among the sea foam, and then I did not see anything more.

I found half an old oar in the bottom of the boat, and somehow or other, after prolonged efforts, I managed to reach the landing. Passing along the shore to my hovel I found myself looking to the side where the blind boy had waited for the nocturnal boatman the night before. The moon was already riding in the sky, and it seemed to me as if some-one in white was sitting on the water's edge. I crept toward the place, driven by curiosity, and lay down in the grass on the cliff overlooking the shore; by pushing my head out a little I had a good view from the crag of everything going on below, and I was very surprised and almost happy to recognize my mermaid. She was wringing the sea foam out of her long hair; the wet blouse outlined her supple waist and high breasts. Soon a boat appeared in the dis-tance and quickly drew near; as on the night before, a man in a Tatar cap stepped out of it, but his hair was cropped like a Cossack's and a large knife was stuck in his leather belt. "Yanko," she said, "all is lost!" Their conversation continued after this but so quietly that I could hear nothing of it. "But where is the blind one?" Yanko said at last, raising his voice. "I sent him off," was the reply. Several minutes later the blind one did appear carrying a sack on his back which he put in the boat.

"Listen to me, blind one," said Yanko, "you guard that place . . . you know the one? There are rich wares there. . . . Tell" (I did not hear the name) "that I am no longer his servant. Things have gone badly and he won't see me anymore. It's dangerous now. I'm going to look for work somewhere else, and he's not going to be able to find such a daring fellow as me. And tell him, if he had paid better for the work, Yanko wouldn't have left him; but my road lies anywhere, where the wind blows and the sea roars." After a certain silence Yanko continued: "She is coming with me; she must not stay here. And tell the old woman that it is time to die, as they say; she has lived long and she must not expect more. She will not see us again."

"And me?" said the blind boy in a plaintive voice.

"What do I want you for?" came the answer.

Meanwhile my mermaid leaped into the boat and waved to her comrade; he put something in the blind boy's hand, adding, "There, buy yourself some gingerbread." "That's all?" said the blind boy. "Well, then, here's some more for you," and coins tinkled as they fell on the stones. The blind boy did not pick them up. The wind was blowing from the shore; Yanko sat down in the boat, hoisted a little sail, and they set off briskly. For a long time the white sail gleamed amidst the dark waves by the light of the moon. The blind boy still sat on the shore, and I heard something like sobbing: the blind boy was really crying, and for a long, long time. . . . I began to feel sad. Why should fate have cast me into a peaceful circle of *honest smugglers*? Like a stone thrown into a smooth pool, I had disturbed their peace, and like a stone, I myself had very nearly gone to the bottom!

I returned home. In the hallway the low-burning candle flickered on the wooden plate, and my Cossack, in spite of my orders, was sleeping a deep sleep, cradling his musket in both arms. I left him in peace, took the candle, and went into the hut. Alas! my traveling box, the saber with the silver mounting, the Daghestan dagger—a gift from a friend—had all disappeared. It was then that I guessed what the things were that that damned blind boy had been carrying. Rousing my Cossack with quite a rude shove, I scolded him, became angry, but there was nothing I could do about it. Would it not have been ludicrous to have complained to the authorities that a blind boy had robbed me and that an eighteen-year-old girl had very nearly drowned me? Thank goodness the opportunity came next morning to go, and I left Taman. I do not know what became of the old woman and the poor blind boy. Anyway, what have the joys and tribulations of mankind to do with me, an itinerant officer, and one traveling on official business to boot!

Princess Mary

Yesterday I arrived in Pyatigorsk and rented rooms on the outskirts of the town, at its highest part, at the foot of Mount Mashuk. When there is a storm, the clouds will come right down to my roof. Just now, at five o'clock in the morning, when I opened the window my room was filled with the scent of flowers which grow in the modest little front garden. Boughs of flowering cherry look in at me through the window, and from time to time the wind scatters their white petals over my writing table. I have a marvelous view in three directions. To the west, five-peaked Beshtu looms dark blue like "the last cloud of dispersing storm." Mashuk rises up like a shaggy Persian cap and covers the entire nothern part of the horizon. In the east the outlook is more cheerful: down below me is the trim, spotless, colorful little town, and the noise from the medicinal springs, the chatter of the polyglot crowd. Farther away the mountains become darker and mistier, rising in a semicircle. And, at the very edge of the horizon, there stretches the silver chain of snowy peaks which starts at Kazbek and ends at Elborus with its twin summits.

What a joy it is to live in such a land! A kind of

comforting feeling runs right through my veins. The air is as clean and fresh as the kiss of a child; the sun is bright, the sky clear blue—what more could one ask for? Why should passions, ambitions, and regrets exist here? But it is time for me to get on. I am going to the Elizavyetinski spring: they say that all the spa's society meets there in the morning.

.   .   .   .

I went down into the center of the town and walked along the boulevard passing several sad-looking groups of people who were slowly climbing up the mountain. For the most part they were the families of steppe landowners. One could tell this immediately by the husbands' well-worn, old-fashioned frock coats and the elaborate apparel of the wives and daughters. Obviously they knew all the young spa people, for they looked at me with a fond curiosity. The St. Petersburg cut of my coat deceived them, but quickly noting my army epaulettes they turned away in disdain.

The wives of the local notables, the spa hostesses, so to speak, are better disposed. They have lorgnettes, pay less attention to uniforms, and are used in the Caucasus to finding ardent hearts behind regimental buttons and an educated mind under a white peaked cap. These ladies are gracious and long-suffering! Every year they have different admirers, and here, perhaps, lies the secret of their perennial courtesy. Climbing up the narrow path to the Elizavyetinski spring, I overtook a crowd of men, civilian and military, who, as I found out later, form a particular class of people among the hopeful traffic of the spa. They drink, but not water; they walk little, hang about without any real purpose; they gamble and complain of the boredom. They are the dandies. They adopt academic poses as they lower their wicker-covered glasses into the well of sulfurous water. The civilians wear bright blue cravats and the soldiers allow frills to show outside their collars. They profess deep contempt for the provincial houses and sigh for the aristocratic drawing rooms of the capital where they are not accepted.

There was the well at last. On the open space nearby a small building with a red roof had been constructed over the baths, and farther on, a gallery where people walk when it rains. A few wounded officers had picked up their crutches and were sitting on a bench looking pale and miserable. Several ladies were walking briskly up and down the courtyard waiting for the waters to take their effect. There were two or three pretty faces among them. Now and again in the walks lined with vines that covered the slope of Mashuk, a colorful bonnet would appear for a moment. It would belong to some lady who liked to be alone—with someone, for I invariably noticed a peaked army cap or a shapeless round hat beside each such bonnet. Lovers of views stood out on a steep cliff, where they have built a pavilion called the Aeolian Harp, and were training a telescope on Elborus. Among them were two tutors and their pupils who had come to be cured of scrofula.

I stopped, out of breath, on the top of the hill, leaned against the corner of the little building, and had begun to survey the picturesque surroundings when suddenly I heard a familiar voice behind me: "Pechorin! How long have you been here?"

I turned around; it was Grushnitski. We embraced each other. I had got to know him in a unit on active service. He had been wounded in the leg by a bullet and had left for the spa a week before me.

Grushnitski is a cadet. He has only been in the

army a year and wears a thick soldier's cloak in a particularly dandyish way. He holds the St. George's military cross. He is well-built, swarthy, and dark-haired. To look at him you might think him twenty-five, although he is hardly twenty-one. He throws his head back when he talks and is always twirling his moustache with his left hand, for his right rests on a crutch. He talks quickly and in an affected way. He is one of those people who have pompous phrases ready for all occasions in life, who are simply not touched by beauty but who cloak themselves sol-emnly in unusual feelings, lofty passions, and ex-clusive sufferings. They like making an effect. The romantic ladies of the provinces like them to distraction. As they get older they become either quiet landowners or else drunkards, and sometimes both. They often have many fine qualities, but not an ounce of poetry. Grushnitski has a passion for declaiming. As soon as a conversation leaves the realm of ordinary ideas, he will smother you with words. I could never argue with him. He does not answer your objections; he does not even listen to you. As soon as you stop talking, he starts a long tirade which seems to have some connection with what you have been saying, but which in fact is mere-ly a continuation of his own speech. He is quite witty. His epigrams are often funny but never pointed or spiteful. He cannot crush anybody with a word. He does not understand people or their weak-nesses because throughout his life he has been con-cerned only with himself. He wants to become the hero of a novel. He has tried so frequently to assure other people that he was not made for this world, that he is doomed by secret sufferings, that he has almost convinced himself of it. That is why he wears his thick soldier's cloak so proudly. I understand him and he does not like me for it, although outwardly we are on the friendliest terms. Grushnitski is reputed to be an outstandingly brave man. I have seen him in action; he waves his saber, shouts, and rushes forward screwing up his eyes. That is not Russian bravery.

I do not like him either. I feel that one day we shall collide on a narrow road and one of us will come to no good.

His arrival in the Caucasus is also a result of his romantic fanaticism. I am sure that on the eve of his departure from the parental village he adopted a tragic look and told some pretty neighbor or other that he was not going simply to serve but that he was seeking death because . . . here he must have covered his eyes with his hands and continued thus: "No, you must not know the reason why! Your pure heart would shudder! What is the point anyway? What am I to you? Do you understand me?" and so on.

He would tell me himself that the motive which made him join the K—— regiment would remain an eternal secret between the heavens and himself.

By the way, in those moments when he discards his tragic mantle, Grushnitski is quite nice and amusing. I am curious to see him with women: I think he has ambitions in that direction.

We greeted each other like old friends. I began to question him about the life at the spa and about the outstanding personalities.

"We lead quite a prosaic life," he said, sighing, "we take the waters in the morning and behave indolently, like all ailing people, and we drink wine in the evening and act insufferably, like all healthy people. Female society exists, but it provides little consolation. They play whist, dress badly, and talk the most terrible French. This year there's only Princess Ligovskoi and her daughter from

Moscow; but I'm not acquainted with them. My soldier's cloak is like the mark of an outcast. The sympathy it arouses is as clumsy as charity."

At that moment two ladies walked past us toward the well. One was elderly, the other quite young and slim. I could not quite see their faces behind their hats, but they were dressed according to the strict rules of the best taste: nothing overdone. The second lady wore a high-necked pearl-gray dress and a light silk scarf was wound around her slender neck. Little boots, puce colored, hugged the ankles of her slim little feet so prettily that even one unordained in the mysteries of beauty would have had to gasp with surprise. Her light but well-bred bearing had something virginal about it which eluded definition but was recognizable at a glance. As she went by, I was conscious of a delicate perfume, such as clings to a letter from a beautiful woman.

"That's Princess Ligovskoi," said Grushnitski, "and that's her daughter with her, Mary, as she calls her à l'anglaise. They've been here only three days."

"And you already know her name?"

"Yes, I heard it by chance," he replied, blushing. "I must confess I don't want to meet them. That proud woman seems to think we soldiers are savages. What's it to them if there's a mind under a numbered cap and a heart beneath a thick cloak?"

"Poor cloak!" I said laughing. "But who's that gentleman going up to them so obligingly and handing them glasses?"

"Oh, that's Rayevich, a dandy from Moscow! He's a gambler: you can tell that straightaway by that huge gold chain wound around his sky-blue waistcoat. and what a thick cane—just like Robinson Crusoe's! Yes, and the beard too, and the haircut à la moujik."

"You bear a grudge against all mankind."

"And there's a reason . . ."

"Oh, really?"

At that moment the ladies walked away from the well and came past us. Grushnitski managed to adopt a dramatic pose with the aid of his crutch and answered me loudly in French:

"Mon cher, je hais les hommes pour ne pas les mépriser, car autrement la vie serait une farce trop dégoûtante."

The exquisite young princess turned around and cast a long inquisitive glance at the speaker. The expression was quite vague but not disdainful, for which I congratulated him inwardly from my heart.

"This Princess Mary is very pretty," I told him. "She has such velvety eyes—really velvety. I advise you to adopt this expression when you talk about her eyes. Her eyelashes are so long that her pupils don't even reflect the sun's rays. I love those lusterless eyes: they're so soft they seem to caress you. Her face seems quite pretty too. . . . And aren't her teeth white, eh? That's most important. It's a pity she didn't smile at your splendid sentence."

"You talk about a pretty woman as if she were an English horse," said Grushnitski indignantly.

"Mon cher," I answered him, trying to imitate his tone, *"je méprise les femmes pour ne pas les aimer, car autrement la vie serait un mélodrame trop ridicule."*

I turned around and walked away from him. For half an hour I strolled through the avenues of vines, between the cliffs and rocks overgrown with bushes. It was beginning to get hot, and I hurried for home. Passing the sulfur spring, I stopped near the covered gallery in order to rest in its shade, and it gave me the opportunity to witness quite a curious scene. The characters were arranged as follows: The old princess and the Moscow dandy were sitting on a bench in the covered gallery, and both seemed to be engaged in serious conversation. The young princess, who had presumably finished her last glass, was walking about near the well, deep in thought. Grushnitski was standing right by the well. No one else was about.

I went nearer and hid behind a corner of the gallery. At that moment Grushnitski dropped his glass on the gravel and tried hard to bend down in order to pick it up, but his injured leg prevented him. Poor chap! How he did try, leaning on his crutch, and all in vain. His expressive face really conveyed suffering.

Princess Mary saw all this better than I did.

She swept over to him lighter than a bird, bent down, picked up the glass, and gave it to him with a gesture full of a charm beyond expression. Then she blushed very red, looked around toward the gallery, and deciding that her mamma had not seen anything, immediately calmed down. When Grushnitski opened his mouth to thank her, she was already far away. A minute later she came out of the gallery with her mother and the dandy, but as she passed by Grushnitski, she adopted a terribly staid and haughty look—did not even turn around or even notice his enamored gaze, which followed her for a long time until, going down the mountain, she was hidden by the lindens of the boulevard. . . . But then her bonnet appeared for a moment across the street. She ran inside the gates of one of the best houses in Pyatigorsk. The old princess went through after her and took her leave of Rayevich at the gate.

Only then did the poor, passionate cadet notice that I was there.

"Did you see?" he asked squeezing my arm; "She's simply an angel!"

"Why?" I asked with a look of purest innocence.

"Didn't you see?"

"Yes, I saw. She picked up your glass. If the keeper had been there, he'd have done just the same, and more quickly too, in the hope of a tip. But then I can understand why she felt sorry for you—you pulled such a terrible face when you stepped on your wounded foot . . ."

"Weren't you at all touched to see her at that moment with her soul shining in her face?"

"No."

I lied, but I wanted to annoy him. I have a born propensity to contradict. My whole life has been merely a succession of miserable and unsuccessful denials of my feelings or reason. The presence of an enthusiast scalds me with a January cold, and I think that frequent contact with a dull phlegmatic person would have made me a passionate dreamer. I further confess that an unpleasant but familiar sensation ran lightly through me at that moment. It was envy. I say "envy" boldly because I am used to being honest with myself about everything. And after all, there is hardly a young man who, meeting a pretty woman who arrests his attention and who suddenly and publicly singles out another man, equally unknown to her for her attentions—there is hardly a young man, I say, who would not find this unpleasant (presuming he mixes in society and is used to indulging his pride).

Grushnitski and I descended the mountain in silence and walked along the boulevard past the windows of the house into which our paragon had vanished. She was sitting by a window. Grushnitski tugged my arm and threw her one of those sloppy-tender glances which have so little effect on women. I trained my lorgnette on her and noticed that whereas she smiled at his glance, my insolent eye-glass had made her really angry. And, indeed, how dare a soldier of the Caucasus point an eye-glass at a Muscovite princess?

13th May

The doctor called on me this morning. His name is Werner, but he is a Russian. What is surprising about that? I once knew an Ivanov who was a German.

Werner is a remarkable man in many ways. Like almost all medical men, he is a skeptic and a materialist, but he is a poet as well, seriously—always a poet in deeds and often in words, although he has not written two verses in his life. He has studied the whole gamut of the human heart, as people study the veins of a corpse. But, just as sometimes a distinguished anatomist cannot cure a fever, he has never been able to make use of his knowledge! Werner usually laughs at his patients on the sly, but I once saw him weep over a dying soldier. . . . He is poor, dreams of millions, but would not go an extra step for money. He once told me that he would rather do a favor for an enemy than a friend, because that would have meant selling his charity, whereas hatred only increased in proportion to an enemy's magnanimity. He has an evil tongue. Many a good soul has been branded a fool by his epigrams. His competitors, the envious spa medical men, spread a rumor that he drew caricatures of his patients—the patients were furious and they almost all left him. His friends, that is, all the really respectable people serving in the Caucasus, tried in vain to restore his falling credit.

His appearance is of a kind which at first sight appears disagreeable, but which one finds pleasing later on, when one has learned to read the marks of a tried and lofty soul in the irregular features.

There have been instances of women falling passionately in love with men like that—women who would not have exchanged that ugliness for the beauty of the freshest and rosiest Endymion. One must give women their due—they have an instinct for spiritual beauty. Perhaps that is why men like Werner love women so passionately.

Werner is short, thin, and as weak as a baby. Like Byron, one of his legs is shorter than the other. By comparison with his trunk, his head seems immense. He wears his hair cropped, and the unevenness of his skull which is thus laid bare would amaze a phrenologist with its strange plexus of conflicting tendencies. His small black eyes are always restless and try to penetrate your thoughts. His clothes are noticeably tasteful and neat. His small, emaciated, veiny hands flaunt bright yellow gloves. His frock coat, cravat, and waistcoat are invariably black. The young people have dubbed him Mephistopheles. He pretends to be annoyed at this nickname but is in fact flattered by it. We soon understood one another and became fairly friendly—for I am not capable of close friendship: of two close friends, one is always the slave of the other, although frequently neither of them will admit it. I cannot be a slave, and to command in such circumstances is a tiresome business, because one must deceive at the same time. Besides, I have servants and money! This is how we became friendly: I met Werner in S—— among a large and noisy group of young people. Toward the end of the evening, the conversation turned to philosophy and metaphysics. People were talking about beliefs, and everyone believed in different things.

"As far as I am concerned, I am sure only of one thing," said the doctor.

"What's that?" I asked, anxious to learn the opinion of a man who had not spoken up till then.

"That sooner or later," he replied, "one fine day I shall die . . ."

"I'm better off than you are," I said, "I have another conviction besides that—namely, one miserable night I had the misfortune to be born."

Everyone thought we were talking nonsense, but in fact none of them said anything cleverer. From that moment we marked each other out in the crowd. We met frequently and spoke very seriously to each other about abstract subjects until we both realized that we were deceiving each other. Then looking each other gravely in the eye, like the Roman augurs did, according to Cicero, we would start to laugh and, having laughed, would part, content with our evening.

I was lying on the sofa with my hands clasped behind my head, looking at the ceiling, when Werner came into my room. He put his walking stick in the corner, sat down in the armchair, yawned, and announced that it was getting hot outside. I replied that the flies were disturbing me—and we both fell silent.

"Take note, my dear doctor," I said, "that without fools this world would be a very boring place. . . . Look, here we are, two intelligent people. We know beforehand that we can argue endlessly about everything, and so we don't argue. We know almost all each other's most intimate thoughts. For us, one word tells a whole story. We can detect the substance of our every feeling through a threefold veil. To us, the sad is funny and the funny, sad, and in any case, if we were to be quite honest, we're pretty well indifferent to everything except ourselves. And so there can't be an exchange of feelings and thoughts between us. We each know what we want to know about the other, and we know more than we want to.

There's only one thing we can do—gossip. Now tell me some news or other."

Fatigued by this long speech, I closed my eyes and yawned. . . . He thought for a moment and then said:

"But there's an idea behind your rigmarole."

"Two!" I retorted.

"You tell me the first and I'll tell you the second."

"All right, you start," I said and continued to survey the ceiling, smiling inwardly.

"You want to know certain details about someone who has come here for the waters, and I have already guessed who it is you are concerned about, because they have already asked about you there."

"Doctor! We really mustn't talk. We read each other's souls."

"Now for the second . . ."

"This is the second idea. I wanted to make you talk about something, because in the first place listening is less tiring: in the second place, one cannot let the cat out of the bag; thirdly, one might find out someone else's secret; fourthly, clever people like you prefer listeners to talkers. Now to business; what did old Princess Ligovskoi tell you about me?"

"Are you so sure it was the old princess . . . and not Princess Mary?"

"Absolutely convinced."

"How?"

"Because the young princess was asking about Grushnitski."

"You have a great gift for putting two and two together. The young princess said that she was sure that the young man in the soldier's cloak had been reduced to the ranks because of a duel . . ."

"I hope you left her with that pleasant delusion."

"Of course."

"Here's a situation," I cried out with delight. "We shall appear in the last act of this comedy. Fate is clearly concerned that I shouldn't be bored."

"I have a feeling," said the doctor, "that poor Grushnitski will be your victim . . ."

"Go on, doctor."

"The old princess said that she knew your face. I suggested that she must have met you in St. Petersburg somewhere in society. I told her your name. . . . She knew it. Evidently your history created quite a stir there. The princess began to talk about your adventures, very likely adding her own observations to the society gossip. . . . Her daughter listened with interest. You have become a hero of a new-style novel in her imagination. I didn't contradict the princess though I knew she was talking nonsense."

"My worthy friend," I said, stretching my hand out toward him. The doctor shook it warmly and continued:

"I'll introduce you, if you like . . ."

"My dear fellow," I said, throwing up my arms, "are heroes introduced? They don't become acquainted except by saving the loved one from certain death."

"So you really want to court the young princess?"

"On the contrary, quite the contrary! . . . Doctor, I have triumphed at last—you don't understand me! But, you know it distresses me, Doctor," I continued after a moment's silence, "although I never reveal my secrets, I'm terribly anxious that they should be discovered because in that way I can always deny them when the occasion arises. But you must describe the mother and daughter to me. What sort of people are they?"

"First of all, the mother is a woman of about forty-five," answered Werner; "she has an excellent stomach, but her blood's bad—red spots on her cheeks. She's spent the last half of her life in Moscow, where she's been inactive and put on weight. She likes suggestive stories and sometimes when her daughter's not in the room, she says indecent things herself. She told me that her daughter's as innocent as a dove. What do I care? I wanted to reply that she might rest assured that I wouldn't tell anyone! The princess is being treated for rheumatism, and the daughter for God knows what. I advised them both to drink two glasses of the sulfur water a day and to take a diluted bath twice a week. The old princess doesn't seem used to wielding authority; she respects her daughter's intelligence and knowledge. Princess Mary has read Byron in English and knows algebra—obviously the young ladies of Moscow have taken to learning, and a very good thing too. Our men are not so very charming on the whole so it must be unbearable for a clever woman to flirt with them. The old princess likes the young people very much but her daughter is rather contemptuous of them—a Moscow habit! They only subsist on forty-year-old wits in Moscow."

"Have you been to Moscow, Doctor?"

"Yes, I had a practice there once."

"Go on."

"I think I've told you everything. Oh! There's one thing more. The daughter seems to like talking about feelings, emotions, and the like. . . . She was in St. Petersburg one winter but she didn't care for it, especially society. I suppose she had a cold reception."

"So you didn't see anyone there today?"

"On the contrary, there was an aide-de-camp, a rather stiff guardsman, and a certain lady—one of the new arrivals—a relation of the old princess through her husband, very good-looking but very ill, apparently. Didn't you meet her at the spring? She's of medium height, blonde, with regular features, and has a consumptive color to her face. There's a black mole on her right cheek. She has an amazingly mobile face."

"A mole!" I muttered through my teeth. "Can it be . . .?"

The doctor looked at me, put his hand on my heart, and said triumphantly:

"You know her! . . ." My heart really was beating faster than usual. "Now it's your turn to be congratulated," I said, "but I rely on you not to give me away. I haven't seen her yet, but I'm sure I recognize a woman I loved in the old days from your description. . . . Don't say a word to her about me; if she asks, speak badly of me."

"If you like," said Werner, shrugging his shoulders.

When he left, an awful melancholy came over me. Has fate led us to the Caucasus again, or has she come here on purpose, knowing she would met me? And how shall we meet? . . . And after all, is it really her. My presentiments have never deceived me. The past holds greater sway over me than any man on earth. Any reminder of past sorrow or joy is painful to me and touches off all the old feelings . . . I am a stupid creature: I forget nothing—absolutely nothing.

After dinner, around six o'clock, I went on to the boulevard. There was a crowd there. The princesses were sitting on a bench surrounded by young people, who were vying with each other to pay them compliments. I took up a position a little way away on another bench, stopped two officers of the D——— regiment whom I knew, and began to talk to them. What I said was obviously funny because they started to laugh like madmen. Curiosity brought several people of the princesses' circle over to me. Gradually they all deserted them and joined my group. I did not stop talking. My anecdotes were clever to the point of foolishness, my sneers at the passersby were spiteful to the point of violence. I continued to amuse my public until the sun went down. Several times the young princess passed nearby on her mother's arm, accompanied by a lame old man. Several times she looked at me, and her glance expressed chagrin while trying to show indifference. . . .

"What was he telling you?" she asked one of the young men who had the courtesy to return to her; "it must have been a very interesting story—his exploits in battle?" She said this quite loudly and with the clear intention of stinging me. Aha, I thought, you are really angry, dear princess; just wait—you will have greater cause.

Grushnitski dogged her footsteps like a beast of prey and did not take his eyes off her for a moment. I wager that tomorrow he will ask someone to introduce him to the old princess. She will be very glad because she is bored.

16th May

During the last two days my affairs have progressed tremendously well. Princess Mary definitely hates me. I have already heard two or three epigrams about me, quite sharp, but also very flattering. She thinks it very strange that as a person used to good society and so intimate with her cousins and aunts in St. Petersburg, I do not try to make her acquaintance. We meet every day by the well and on the boulevard. I use all my powers to attract her admirers away from her, the glittering aides-de-camp, the pale Muscovites, and the rest, and almost always succeed. I always hated entertaining, but now my house is full every day. They dine, sup, play cards—and alas, my champagne prevails over the power of her magnetic eyes.

I met her yesterday in Chelakhov's shop. She was bargaining for a splendid Persian rug. The princess was urging her mamma not to be stingy, that rug would look so nice in her room! I paid forty rubles more and bought it myself. For that I was rewarded with a blazing look of the most enrapturing fury. About dinner time I purposely had my Circassian horse covered with the rug and led past her windows. Werner was there at the time and told me that the effect was most dramatic. The princess is preaching a crusade against me. I have even noticed that two aides-de-camp acknowledge me very dryly when she is about even though they dine with me every day.

Grushnitski has adopted a mysterious look. He walks about with his hands thrust behind his back and recognizes no one. His leg has suddenly got better—he hardly limps at all. He has found an opportunity to enter into conversation with the old princess and pay some compliment to her daughter. She is obviously not very fastidious, for since then she answers his bow with the kindest of smiles.

"D'you really not want to meet the Ligovskois?" he asked me yesterday.

"Certainly not!"

"My dear fellow! It's the most agreeable house at the spa! The cream of local society . . ."

"My friend, I'm bored with the cream of any society. But do you go there?"

"Not yet. I have spoken twice to the young princess, not more. You know, somehow I feel awkward about intruding into their house, even though it's what is done here. . . . It would be another matter if I wore epaulettes."

"For pity's sake! You are much more interesting as you are. You just don't know how to exploit your advantages. That soldier's cloak makes you a hero and a martyr in the eyes of every sensitive young lady."

Grushnitski smiled proudly. "What nonsense!" he said.

"I'm sure," I continued, "that Princess Mary is already in love with you."

He blushed to the roots of his hair and puffed himself up.

Oh pride! Thou lever with which Archimedes tried to raise the globe . . .

"You're full of jokes," he said, pretending to be annoyed, "in the first place, she doesn't know me well enough yet."

"Women only love those they don't know."

"But I have absolutely no pretensions to be liked by her. I simply want to get to know an agreeable household. It would be quite ridiculous if I had any hopes of . . . Now, you, for instance, you're another matter! You St. Petersburg lions: you just have to look and women melt. . . . But do you know what the young princess was saying about you, Pechorin?"

"What? Has she spoken to you about me?"

"Don't be too pleased. Somehow or other I got into conversation with her by the well. One of the first things she said was, 'Who is that gentleman who has much an unpleasant, heavy look? He was with you when . . .' She blushed when she remembered her kind escapade; she didn't want to refer to the occasion. 'You need not say it,' I replied, 'I shall always remember . . .' My friend, Pechorin, I don't congratulate you. She has a poor opinion of you. . . . I'm really sorry. Because my Mary's very sweet. . ."

I must remark that Grushnitski is one of those

people who, when they talk of a woman they hardly know but who has had the good fortune to please them, call her *my Mary, my Sophie*.

I looked serious and answered him:

"Yes, she's not bad-looking. . . . But take care, Grushnitski. Most Russian ladies feed only on platonic love and don't entertain any thoughts of marriage. And platonic love is the most disturbing kind. The princess seems to be one of those women who likes to be amused. If she's bored with you for two minutes on end, you'll be lost forever. Your silence should arouse her curiosity, but your conversation will never satisfy her completely. You must keep her guessing all the time. She'll disregard opinion publicly a dozen times for your sake, but she'll call it sacrifice, and to compensate herself for it she'll begin to torture you, and afterward she'll simply say that she can't bear you. If you don't keep the upper hand, then even her first kiss won't give you the right to a second. She'll flirt with you to her heart's content and in two years she'll marry a monster, out of obedience to her mother. Then she'll assure you that she's unhappy, that she only ever loved one man—that is, you—but that heaven didn't want to join them together, because he wore a soldier's cloak, although under that thick gray cloak there beat a noble and passionate heart . . ."

Grushnitski banged his fist on the table and started to walk up and down the room.

I was laughing to myself, and even smiled once or twice, but fortunately he did not notice. He is obviously in love, because he is more credulous than he was. He has even appeared with a silver ring inlaid with black, a local product. It looked suspicious to me . . . I began to examine it, and what did I find? The name "Mary" was engraved in small letters on the inside and beside it the date on which she picked up the celebrated glass. I concealed my discovery. I do not want to force confessions out of him. I want him to single me out for his confidences—and then I shall enjoy myself.

. . . .

I got up late today. I arrived at the well, but no one was there yet. It was getting hot; shaggy white clouds were running swiftly away from the snowy mountains, promising a storm. Mashuk's summit was smoking like a dowsed torch. Around it, gray shreds of cloud, halted in their course, were creeping and winding about like snakes, and seemed to catch themselves on the spinous shrubbery. The air was full of electricity. I went deeper into the avenue of vines which lead to the grotto. I felt sad. I was thinking of the young woman with the mole on her cheek whom the doctor had been speaking about. . . . Why was she here? And was it really her? And why did I think that it was her? And why was I even so sure of this? Are there so few women with moles on their cheeks? Thinking these thoughts, I walked right up to the grotto itself. In the shade of its vault I saw a woman sitting on a stone bench. She wore a straw bonnet and was wrapped in a black shawl. She was hanging her head and her face was hidden behind a bonnet. I was about to turn away so as not to disturb her meditation when she caught sight of me.

"Vera!" I cried involuntarily.

She was startled and turned rather white.

"I knew you were here," she said. I sat down beside her and took her hand. A long-forgotten tremor ran through my veins at the sound of that sweet voice. Her deep, calm eyes looked into mine.

They reflected mistrust and something akin to a reproach.

"We haven't seen each other for a long time," I said.

"A long time, and we've both changed a great deal."

"So you don't love me?"

"I'm married," she said.

"Again? But you had that excuse a few years ago, and it didn't prevent . . ."

She shook her hand out of mine, and her cheeks blazed up.

"Perhaps you love your second husband?"

She did not reply and turned away.

"Or is he very jealous?"

Silence.

"What then? He's young, good-looking, and very rich, I suppose, and you're afraid . . ." I looked at her and became frightened. Her face reflected deep despair, tears were shining in her eyes.

"Tell me," she whispered at last, "does it make you so happy to torture me? I ought to hate you. Ever since the day we met you have given me nothing but suffering . . ." Her voice was shaking. She leaned toward me and buried her head in my breast.

"Perhaps that's why you loved me," I thought, "joys are forgotten, but never misery . . ."

I held her tightly in my arms, and we stayed like that for a long time. At last our lips were drawn together and merged into a hot, transporting kiss. Her hands were as cold as ice; her head was burning. Then one of those conversations started between us which are meaningless on paper, which one cannot repeat or even remember exactly, for the tones and cadences change and heighten the meaning of the words, as they do in an Italian opera.

She definitely does not want me to make the acquaintance of her husband—that lame old man whom I saw for a moment on the boulevard. She married him for her son's sake. He is rich and suffers from rheumatism. I did not allow myself one sneer at him. She respects him as a father—and will deceive him as a husband. . . . The human heart is a strange thing, and woman's in particular!

Vera's husband, Semyon Vassilyevich G——, is a distant relative of Princess Ligovskoi's. He is living next door to her. Vera is often at the princess's, and I promised her that I would make the Ligovskois' acquaintance and pay court to the young princess so as to draw attention away from her. In this way my plans have not been in the least upset, and it will give me great pleasure . . .

Pleasure! But I have already passed that time of life when one seeks only happiness, when one feels it essential to love someone intensely and passionately—now I only want to be loved, and that by very few. I even think that a single permanent attachment would be enough for me: pitiable human trait . . .

I have always thought one thing strange. I have never become a slave to any woman—on the contrary, without ever trying to do so, I have always possessed an irresistible power over them. Why is this?—why is it that I have never really set much value on anything, why is it that they have always been afraid of losing me? Is it the magnetic influence of a strong organism, or just that I never happened to meet a stubborn woman?

I must admit that I do not like women of character really: but that is their worry.

I remember now: it is true that once, and only once, I did love a woman who was strong-willed, and I never managed to conquer her. We parted enemies—but then, perhaps if I had met her five years later, we would have parted otherwise.

Vera is ill, very ill, although she will not admit it. I am afraid that she has consumption or that disease which is called *fièvre lente*—not a Russian disease at all, and it has no name in our language.

The storm caught us in the grotto and kept us there for another half hour. She did not make me swear fidelity, did not inquire if I had loved others since we parted. She committed herself to me again with her old lack of caution—and I shall not deceive her. She is the only woman in the world whom I have not the power to deceive. I know that we shall soon be parted again forever, perhaps, and we shall both go on to the grave by different paths. But her memory will remain sacred to me. I always told her this and she believes me, although she says she does not.

We separated at last, and I watched her for a long time, until her bonnet disappeared behind the bushes and rocks. My heart contracted painfully, as it did after the first separation. Oh, how I rejoiced in that feeling! Can youth with its generous storms be wanting to return to me, or is it only its farewell glance, a last gift—to be remembered by? But it is comic to think that in appearance I am still a boy. Although my face is pale, it is still fresh; my limbs are supple and slender; thick curls of hair grow on my head; my eyes blaze; my blood runs swiftly.

When I returned home, I mounted and rode out onto the steppe. I love riding a spirited horse through the long grass against a desert wind. I gulp the fragrant air hungrily and strain my eyes into the dark-blue distance, trying to catch the misty outlines of objects, which become clearer and clearer with every moment. No matter what grief oppresses one's spirit or what unrest exhausts one's thoughts, it all disperses in a moment. One's heart lightens, and the body's weariness overcomes the mind's alarm. There is not a woman's glance I would not forget at the sight of the curving mountains, lit by the southern sun, at the sight of the bright-blue sky, or hearing the sound of a torrent falling from crag to crag.

I think that the Cossacks, peering from their watchtowers, and seeing me riding about without aim or object, were very puzzled for they must have taken me for a Circassian by my clothes. In fact I have been told that when I am in Circassian costume and on horseback, I am more like a Kabardin than many Kabardins. And really, I am a complete dandy when it comes to the noble warlike dress. Just the right amount of lace, costly weapons in simple settings, the fur on the cap neither too long nor too short; leggings and boots fitted with greatest possible exactness; a long white tunic and a dark-brown Circassian coat. I spent a long time learning the way the mountain people ride: not to flatter my self-esteem so much as to assess my skill in riding in the Caucasian style. I own four horses: one for myself and three for my friends so that I should not be bored riding alone. They are happy to take my horses, but they never ride with me. It was already six o'clock in the afternoon when I remembered that it was time for dinner. My horse was tired, and I rode out onto the road which leads from Pyatigorsk to the "German colony" where spa society often goes for a picnic. The road winds between bushes and down small gullies where noisy streams run shaded by the high grass. All around, the dark-blue masses —Beshtu, the Snake, Iron, and Bald mountains rise up to form an amphitheater. I rode down into one of these gullies, called "dells" in the local dialect, and stopped to water my horse. At that moment a noisy, glittering cavalcade appeared on the road—

ladies in black and sky-blue riding habits, gentlemen in costumes consisting of a mixture of Circassian and provincial. Grushnitski and Princess Mary were riding in front.

The ladies at the spa still believed that the Circassians attack in broad daylight. This was probably the reason why Grushnitski was wearing a saber and a pair of pistols over his soldier's cloak. He looked quite ridiculous in these heroic vestments. A high bush hid me from them, but I could see everything through the leaves and I gathered from the expression on their faces that the conversation was sentimental. At last they approached the descent. Grushnitski took the princess's horse by the bridle, and then I heard the end of their conversation:

"And you want to stay in the Caucasus for the rest of your life?" the princess was saying.

"What's Russia to me?" replied her escort, "a country where thousands of people look at me with contempt because they are richer than I am. But here—well, this thick cloak didn't prevent my meeting you here . . ."

"On the contrary," said the princess, blushing.

Grushnitski's face showed pleasure. He continued:

"Here my life passes noisily, swiftly, and unnoticed, under the savages' bullets, and if God were to send me a bright womanly glance every year, one like . . ."

At that moment they drew level with me. I whipped up my horse and rode out from behind the bush.

"Mon dieu, un circassien," the princess cried out in terror. In order to reassure her I replied in French, bowing slightly: *"Ne craignez rien, madame —je ne suis plus dangereux que votre cavalier."*

She was embarrassed—but why? Because of her mistake, or because my answer seemed impertinent?

I hoped my second supposition was correct. Grushnitski glanced at me with displeasure.

Late that night, about eleven o'clock, I went for a stroll down the lime walks of the boulevard. Lights were burning in only a very few windows; the town was asleep. Crests of precipices rose up blackly on three sides—offshoots of Mashuk, on whose peak lay an ominous cloud. The moon was rising over the east, and in the distance the snow-covered mountains shimmered in a silver fringe. The calls of the sentries alternated with the murmur of the hot springs, which had been allowed to run free for the night. From time to time the tramping of a horse would reverberate down the street accompanied by the creaking of a cart and the plaintive chant of a Tatar. I sat down on a bench overcome by sad thoughts. I felt I had to pour them out to someone sympathetic . . . but who was there? "What's Vera doing now?" I thought. I would have given much to be holding her hand at that moment.

Suddenly I heard swift, uneven steps. . . . It must be Grushnitski . . . and so it was!

"Where have you been?"

"At Princess Ligovskoi's," he said very proudly. "How Princess Mary sings!"

"Do you know what?" I said to him, "I'll bet that she doesn't know that you're a cadet. She thinks you've been reduced to the ranks."

"Perhaps! What does it matter to me?" he said absently.

"No, I only say that to . . ."

"But do you know, you made her terribly angry before? She thought it an unheard-of impertinence. I hardly managed to convince her that you were too well-bred and that you knew society too well to have had any intention of insulting her. She says you look so insolent that you must have the greatest conceit possible."

"She's quite right. . . . But you don't want to take her part, do you?"

"I'm only sorry that I have no right to."

"Aha!" I thought, "he already has hopes then."

"Anyway, it's worse for you," Grushnitski continued, "you'll find it hard to make their acquaintance now. What a pity, it's one of the pleasant . . . houses I know."

I smiled to myself.

"At this moment, the pleasantest house for me is my own," I said, yawning, and stood up to go.

"But you must admit that you're sorry now . . ."

"What nonsense! If I feel so inclined, I shall be at the princess's tomorrow evening."

"We'll see . . ."

"If it gives you pleasure, I'll even start courting the young princess."

"Yes, if she feels like talking to you."

"I'm just waiting for the moment when she gets tired of your conversation. Good-bye!"

"I'm going for a stroll, I won't get to sleep now anyhow. . . . Listen, why don't we go to the restaurant? There's gambling there, and I need stimulation at the moment."

"I hope you lose."

I went home.

21st May

Almost a week has passed, and I still have not become acquainted with the Ligovskois. I am waiting for a suitable occasion. Grushnitski follows Princess Mary everywhere like a shadow. Their conversations are endless. When will she tire of him? Her mother pays no attention to it all because he is not "eligible." There's mothers' logic for you. I have noticed two or three tender looks pass between them. I must put an end to this.

Yesterday Vera appeared at the well for the first time. She had not ventured out since we met in the grotto. We put down our glasses at the same time, and as we bent over, she whispered to me:

"Don't you want to meet the Ligovskois? We can only see each other there."

A reproach, and that is tiresome. But I deserved it.

By the way, there will be a subscription ball tomorrow in the assembly hall, and I shall dance a mazurka with the princess.

22nd May

The restaurant hall was transformed into a meeting place of gentlefolk. Everyone arrived at nine o'clock. The princess and her daughter were among the last to arrive. Not a few ladies looked at her with envy and malice, because Princess Mary dresses with taste. Those who consider themselves the local aristocracy concealed their envy and joined her. How could it be otherwise? Two spheres, an upper and a lower, invariably appear wherever ladies gather. Grushnitski was standing outside by a window with a crowd of people. He was pressing his face to the glass, his eyes glued to his goddess. As she passed, she gave him a barely noticeable nod of her head. He beamed like the sun. The dancing started with a polka, then they played a waltz. Spurs jangled, coattails rose and whirled.

I was standing behind a stout lady who sprouted pink feathers. The fullness of her dress was reminiscent of the era of hooped skirts, and her rough blotchy skin of the happy epoch of beauty spots made of black taffeta. A clasp covered the largest wart on her neck. She was talking to her partner, a captain of dragoons:

"That Princess Ligovskoi is an insufferable hussy.

E

Imagine, she pushed me and didn't apologize, but turned and looked at me through her lorgnette. *C'est impayable.* . . . Why does she think so much of herself? She ought to be taught a lesson."

"That's the least thing we can do," replied the obliging captain and went off into the next room.

I immediately went up to the young princess and, taking advantage of the freedom of local custom which allows one to dance with ladies one does not know, asked her to dance a waltz with me.

She could not quite suppress a smile nor conceal her triumph. However she managed to adopt an air of indifference and even severity quite quickly. She put her hand carelessly onto my shoulder, inclined her head slightly to the side, and we set off. I do not know a waist more alluring and more willowy! I felt her clean breath on my face. Sometimes a curl, shaken free from its companions by a turn in the waltz, brushed against my hot cheek. I made three tours of the room. (She waltzes amazingly well.) She was out of breath, her eyes went dim, her half-opened lips could hardly whisper the necessary:

"Merci, monsieur."

There were a few moments of silence, and then, with an air of great humility, I said:

"Princess, I hear that, although you don't know me, I have already had the misfortune to earn your disfavor, that you find me insolent. . . . Can that be true?"

"Would you like to confirm me in the opinion now?" she retorted with an ironic pout which, incidentally, suits her volatile personality very well.

"If I have had the temerity to offend you in any way, allow me the still greater temerity of asking your forgiveness. . . . I should like very much to prove that you were mistaken about me."

"You will find that rather difficult."

"Why?"

"Because you do not visit us, and I don't think that balls are very frequent here."

That means, I thought, that their doors are closed to me forever.

I was rather annoyed and said:

"You know, Princess, you should never spurn a repentant offender: he may become doubly offensive out of despair, and then . . ."

The laughter and whispering of the people around us made me interrupt my sentence and turn around. A few steps away from me stood a crowd of men, among them the captain of dragoons, who had expressed hostile intentions against the amiable princess. He was obviously very pleased about something, rubbing his hands and laughing and winking to his companions. Suddenly a gentleman in tails, with long moustaches and an ugly red face detached himself from them and directed his uncertain steps toward the princess. He was drunk. He halted opposite the embarrassed princess and, clasping his hands behind his back, fixed her with his gray eyes and pronounced in a hoarse falsetto: "*Permettez* . . . Oh, what's the use. . . . I simply invite you for a mazurka."

"What do you want?" she said in a tremulous voice, casting imploring glances around her. Alas, her mother was a long way off, and there were no escorts whom she knew nearby. One adjutant saw it all apparently, but hid behind a crowd of people so as not to be involved in the affair.

"What's this?" asked the drunken gentleman, winking at the dragoon who was encouraging him by signs, "Don't you want to? I again have the honor to invite you *pour mazure.* . . . Perhaps you think I'm drunk? It's nothing! Much freer, I assure you . . ."

I saw that she was ready to faint with mortification and fear.

I went up to the drunken gentleman, took him quite firmly by the arm, and, looking him steadily in the eye, asked him to go away, because, I added, the princess had promised to dance the mazurka with me a long time ago.

"Oh well, that's that . . . another time then," he said starting to laugh, and walked away to his abashed companions, who immediately led him off into the next room.

I was rewarded with a deep, enchanting look.

The princess went up to her mother and told her everything. The latter sought me out in the crowd and thanked me. She told me that she knew my mother and was on friendly terms with half a dozen of my aunts.

" I don't know how it is that we haven't met until now," she added, "but you must admit you are the only one to blame for that. It's quite unheard of, the way you shun everybody. I hope the atmosphere of my drawing room will drive away your spleen. Isn't that so?"

I said some phrase or other that everyone ought to have ready for occasions such as this.

The quadrilles went on for an incredibly long time.

At last the strains of a mazurka rang out from the gallery. The princess and I sat down.

I did not once allude to the drunken gentleman, to my previous conduct, or to Grushnitski. The impression which the unpleasant scene had made on her gradually dispersed and her little face became animated again. She joked very pleasantly; her conversation was lively, free, and witty without pretension to wit. Her remarks were sometimes deep. In a very involved sentence I made her feel that I had admired her for some time. She bowed her head and blushed.

"You are a strange man," she said afterward, raising her velvety eyes to mine and giving a forced laugh.

"I didn't want to meet you," I continued, "because you're surrounded by too dense a crowd of admirers, and I was afraid I wouldn't be noticed in it."

"You need not have feared that! They are all terribly boring."

"All! Not all of them, surely?"

She looked at me steadily as if trying to remember something, blushed again, and eventually said in a decisive voice: *"All of them!"*

"Even my friend Grushnitski?"

"Is he your friend?" she said, showing some doubt.

"Yes."

"One couldn't classify him as being boring, of course . . ."

"But you could classify him as being unfortunate," I said, laughing.

"Of course! Do you think that's funny? I wish you were in his shoes."

"What? I was a cadet myself once, and to tell you the truth, it was the best time of my life."

"Is he a cadet then?" she asked, quickly, and then added: "But I thought . . ."

"What did you think?"

"Nothing! . . . Who is that lady?"

Here the conversation changed course and did not return to the subject.

Then the mazurka came to an end and we parted —till the next time. The ladies drove away. I went for supper and met Werner.

"Aha," he said, "so it's you! And you didn't want

to meet the princess except by saving her from certain death."

"I did better than that," I answered him, "I saved
her from fainting at the ball."

"How was that? Tell me."

"No, you can guess everything, so guess for yourself!"

23rd May

About seven o'clock this evening I was strolling
along the boulevard when Grushnitski saw me from
a distance and came up to me. His eyes were shining with some absurd sort of delight. He shook my
hand warmly and said in a tragic voice:

"Thank you, Pechorin. Do you understand me?"

"No. But whatever it is it doesn't merit thanks,"
I replied, having absolutely no good deed on my
conscience.

"What? But yesterday! Have you forgotten? Mary
told me everything."

"And so? Have you got everything now? And
gratitude too?"

"Listen," said Grushnitski, very pompously, "if
you want to remain my friend, please stop making
fun of my love. . . . You see, I'm madly in love
with her . . . and I think, I hope, she loves me too.
I've a favor to ask you. You'll be at their reception
this evening, so promise me to take note of everything. I know you're experienced in these things,
you know women better than I do. Women! Women!
Who can understand them? Their smiles contradict
their looks, their words promise and beckon, while
their tones of voice push one away. . . . One minute
they perceive and understand our most secret
thoughts, the next they don't even grasp our most
obvious hints. That's the princess for you. Yesterday her eyes shone with emotion when they fell on
me, now they're dull and cold . . ."

"It's probably the effect of the waters," I replied.

"You see the bad side of everything . . . materialist!" he added, scornfully. "Anyway, we'll change the matter," and, pleased with his bad pun, he cheered up again.

At nine o'clock we went together to the princess's.

Passing Vera's house, I saw her by the window. We cast a fleeting glance at each other. She came into the Ligovskois' drawing room shortly after us. The old princess introduced her to me as a kinswoman. We drank tea. There were many guests, and the conversation was general. I tried to please the old princess, joked and made her laugh wholeheartedly. Princess Mary too wanted to laugh more than once, but she stopped herself so as not to depart from her chosen role. She thinks that languor suits her—and—perhaps she is right. Grushnitski seemed very glad that my gaiety did not infect her.

After tea everyone went into the salon.

"Are you pleased with my obedience, Vera?" I said as I went past her.

She cast me a glance full of love and gratitude. I am used to looks like that now, but at one time they meant ecstasy to me. The princess led her daughter down to the piano. Everybody asked her to sing. I kept silent and, taking advantage of the bustle, walked away toward the window with Vera, who wanted to say something of great importance for both of us. It turned out to be nonsense.

Meanwhile I could tell from one blazingly angry glance that my indifference was annoying the princess. Oh, I understand this dumb language, so expressive, concise, and powerful, remarkably well!

She started to sing. Her voice is quite pleasant, but she sings badly. Anyway, I did not listen. Grushnitski, however, was leaning on the piano, facing her, and was gloating over her, saying, *"Charmant! Délicieux!"* every minute in an undertone.

"Listen," Vera was telling me, "I don't want you to meet my husband, but you mustn't fail to be nice to the old princess. That will be easy for you—you can do anything you want to. We shall only see each other here . . ."

"Only here?"

She blushed and continued:

"You know I'm your slave. I've never been able to resist you . . . and I shall be punished for it. You'll fall out of love with me. But I want to preserve my reputation at least . . . not for my own sake, you know that only too well. Oh, I do beg you not to torture me with groundless suspicions and pretended indifference as you have in the past. I shall probably die soon; I feel weaker every day . . . but I still can't think of the life to come, I can only think of you. You men don't appreciate the pleasures of a look, of the touch of a hand . . . but I'll let you have your way. I feel so deeply, so strangely happy, when I listen to your voice that the most passionate kiss is no substitute for it."

Meanwhile, Princess Mary had stopped singing. A murmur of praise rose around her. I went to her after everyone else and said something rather perfunctory about her voice. She pulled a face, pouted, and gave a mock curtsey.

"That's all the more flattering to me," she said, "since you didn't even listen to me. But perhaps you don't like music?"

"Oh the contrary . . . especially after dinner."

"Grushnitski is right when he says you have the most prosaic tastes . . . and I see that you like music in relation to food."

"You are wrong again. I'm not a gourmet at all: I have the most terrible stomach. But music after

dinner makes one drowsy, and it's healthy to sleep
after dinner, therefore I like music in relation to
health. Late in the evening, on the other hand, it
irritates my nerves too much. It makes me either
sad or too gay. Both are quite tedious when there's
no positive reason to be too sad or gay. Anyway
sadness is ridiculous in society, and too much gaiety
is indecent."

She did not hear me out but walked away and
sat down next to Grushnitski. Some sort of sentimental conversation started up between them.

Although she was trying to appear as if she were
listening to him attentively, the princess seemed to
be answering his wise remarks rather distractedly
and unsuccessfully, because from time to time he
would look at her with surprise, trying to guess the
cause of her inner disturbance, which was reflected
from time to time in her restless look.

But I have your measure, dear Princess, so take
care. You want to pay me back with my own coin,
prick my self-esteem, but you won't succeed. And if
you declare war on me, I shall be merciless.

I tried several times during the course of the evening to break into their conversation, but she received my remarks rather dryly, and at last I went
away, pretending to be angry. The princess had
triumphed; Grushnitski too. Exult, my friends, but
make the most of it . . . your triumph will not last
long! . . . How can I tell that? I have a premoni-
tion. . . . Whenever I have met a woman, I have
always been able to tell if she would love me or
not . . .

I spent the rest of the evening at Vera's side and
talked my fill about the past. I really do not know
why she loves me so much. Especially since she is
a woman who understands me completely and

knows all my petty weaknesses and wicked emotions. Can wickedness be so attractive?

I left with Grushnitski. Outside, he took me by the arm and, after a long silence, said:

"What do you think?"

I wanted to say, "You're a fool," but restrained myself and merely shrugged my shoulders.

29th May

All this time I have not once departed from my plan. The princess is beginning to like my conversation. I told her about several strange incidents in my life, and she is beginning to see me as an unusual man. I ridicule everything in the world, especially feelings, and it is beginning to frighten her. She dare not start sentimental discussions with Grushnitski when I am there and she has answered Grushnitski's jokes with a mocking smile on more than one occasion. But whenever Grushnitski comes near I adopt a meek look and leave them together. She was very pleased at this the first time and tried to show it; the second time she was annoyed with me; the third time with Grushnitski.

"You have a very poor opinion of yourself," she told me yesterday. "Why do you think that I enjoy Grushnitski's company more than yours?"

I replied that I was sacrificing my own pleasure for the happiness of a friend.

"And sacrificing mine too," she added.

I watched her closely and looked serious. After that I did not say a single word to her the whole day. Last night she was thoughtful, this morning at the well she was even more thoughtful. When I went up to her, she was listening absently to Grushnitski, who was admiring nature. But as soon as she noticed me she started to laugh (quite irrelevantly) and pretended she had not noticed me. I moved a little farther off and began to watch her. She turned away from her companion and yawned twice. Grushnitski was definitely boring her. I shall not speak to her for another two days.

3rd June

I often ask myself why I try so hard to get the love of a young girl whom I have no wish to seduce and whom I shall never marry. Why this womanish coquetry? Vera loves me more than Princess Mary will ever love anybody. If I thought she was an unconquerable beauty, then perhaps I might be attracted by the difficulty of the undertaking . . . but that is not the case at all! So it cannot be that restless need for love which tortures us in our early years —that need which throws us from one woman to another until we find one who cannot bear us. At this stage we become constant—with that true and unending passion which one can express mathematically by a line falling from a point into space. The secret of this endlessness lies simply in the impossibility of achieving the objective, that is, the end.

Why am I taking all this trouble? Because I am jealous of Grushnitski? Poor fellow, he certainly has not earned it! Or is it a product of that nasty but uncontrollable feeling which makes us destroy a friend's sweet illusions, merely to obtain the small satisfaction of telling him, when he despairs and asks what he ought to believe, "My friend, I've been through the same thing, and you see that I can still dine, sup, and sleep quite peacefully. And I hope I shall be able to die without screaming or tears!"

There are immense pleasures in possessing a young spirit that has just started to bloom. It is like a little flower whose most delicate scent evaporates on meeting the first ray of the sun. One must pluck it just at that moment and, having breathed in one's fill of it, throw it on the wayside—perhaps someone will pick it up. I feel I have that insatiable hunger which will devour everything that crosses its path. I see the joys and sufferings of others only in relation to myself, I see them as food to sustain my spiritual powers. I myself am no longer capable of acting recklessly under the influence of emotion. My ambition has been choked by obstacles, but it has appeared in another form, namely, as a lust for power. My chief satisfaction is to subject everything around me to my will. Is it not the first sight and the greatest triumph of power to be able to arouse feelings of love, devotion, and fear toward oneself? Is it not the greatest sop to our pride to be the cause of suffering and joy in someone else, without having any positive right to be so? What is happiness but satiated pride? If I had thought myself better and stronger than everyone else in the world, I should be happy. If everyone loved me, I should have found an endless source of love in myself. Evil breeds evil—the first pain makes one understand the satisfaction of torturing others. The idea of evil cannot enter a man's head without his wanting to put it into practice. It has been said that ideas are organic forms: their birth gives them form and that form is action. He who conceives more ideas will act more than others. That is why a genius chained to a clerk's desk must die or go mad, just as a powerfully built man who leads a sedentary life and behaves humbly dies of an apoplectic stroke.

Passions are nothing else but ideas beginning to develop. They belong to one's youth, and he is a fool who thinks he will be disturbed by them all his life. There are many calm rivers which start in noisy waterfalls, but none of them gush and splash right down to the sea. However, the calm is often a sign of great, but hidden powers. Abundance and depth of feelings preclude raging passions. A mind which suffers and is glad renders strict account to itself for everything and is convinced that it should. It knows that if there were no storms, the continual heat of the sun would shrivel it up. It is filled with its own life; it soothes and punishes itself like a favorite child. Only at this highest level of self-knowledge can a man appraise God's justice. As I read through this page I notice that I have been led far away from my subject—but what does it matter? After all, I am writing this journal for myself and so whatever I put into it will be a treasured memory for me in time.

* * * * * * * * * * * *

Grushnitski arrived and threw himself round my neck—he has been commissioned. We drank champagne. Doctor Werner came in after him.

"I can't congratulate you," he told Grushnitski.

"Why not?"

"Because that soldier's cloak suits you very well and you must admit that an infantry officer's uniform made here, at the spa, won't do anything interesting for you. . . . You see, until now you've been the exception, but now you'll be part of the general rule."

"Talk away, talk away, Doctor! You won't stop me rejoicing. He doesn't know," added Grushnitski into my ear, "how many hopes these epaulettes have given me . . . O epaulettes, epaulettes! Your little stars, guiding stars . . . No, now I'm completely happy!"

"Are you coming for a walk to the chine with us?" I asked him.

"Me? I wouldn't let the princess see me for anything until my uniform's ready."

"Do you want us to tell her your good news?"

"No, please don't say anything, I want to surprise her."

"But tell me, how are your affairs progressing with her?"

He was embarrassed at this and started to think. He wanted to boast, to lie, but his conscience pricked him, and at the same time he was ashamed to tell the truth.

"What do you think, does she love you?"

"Love me? My dear Pechorin, what ideas you do have! How can one fall in love so quickly? And even if she did love me, a lady wouldn't say."

"Good! And I suppose you think that a gentleman shouldn't talk about his affections either?"

"Oh, my friend, there's a way of doing everything. There isn't a great deal spoken, it's presumed . . ."

"That's so. But the love we read in the eyes doesn't bind any woman, whereas words. . . . Look out for yourself, Grushnitski, she's cheating you."

"She?" He replied, raising his eyes to heaven and smiling in self-satisfaction, "I feel sorry for you, Pechorin."

He went out.

In the evening a considerable crowd set off to the chine on foot. According to the local scholars, that chine is nothing but an extinct crater. It is situated on a slope of Mashuk, two-thirds of a mile from the town. A narrow path leads up to it between shrubs and rocks. Climbing up, I gave my arm to the princess, and she did not let go of it throughout the walk.

Our conversation started with scandal. I began to dissect those of our acquaintance who were there and those who were not, dwelling on their amusing characteristics at first and, later, on their bad ones.

My bile was stirred. I began in fun and ended with open venom. At first this amused her, but later it frightened her.

"You are a dangerous man," she said to me. "I would rather fall victim to a murderer's knife than your tongue. I beg you in earnest: when you think of speaking badly about me, take a knife and cut my throat instead—I don't think you would find that very difficult."

"Do you really think I'm a murderer?"

"You're worse."

I thought for a moment and then said, pretending to be deeply touched:

"Yes, that was my failing from childhood. Everyone saw bad traits in me, which weren't there; but they presumed that they were—and so they were born. I was meek, and they accused me of craftiness, so I became furtive. I felt good and evil deeply. No one petted me, everyone insulted me, so I became spiteful. I was surly—other children were gay and full of chatter. I felt myself superior to them, but they thought me inferior. I became jealous. I was ready to love the whole world, but no one understood me and so I learned to hate. My miserable youth was spent in a struggle with myself and the world. Afraid of derision, I buried my finer feelings in the depths of my heart and they died there. I told the truth, but people didn't believe me, so I began to practice deception. I had found out about the world and the mainsprings of society, and I became an expert in the science of life. I saw that others were happy without these arts and made free use of the advantages which I had been striving after so untiringly. And then despair was born in me, not that despair which can be cured by the muzzle of a pistol, but a cold, powerless despair screened by courtesy and a good-natured smile. I became a moral cripple. One part of me did not survive; it dried up, evaporated, died. I cut it off and threw it away. Although the other part still functioned and was there for anyone to find, no one noticed it, because no one knew of the existence of the dead half. But you reminded me of it just now, and I have read you its epitaph. Epitaphs seem to amuse some people, but not me, especially when I remember what lies beneath them. Anyway, I don't ask you to share my opinion. If what I have said seems funny to you, please laugh. I can tell you in advance that it won't annoy me in the least."

I met her eyes at that moment. They were filled with tears. Her hand, which was resting in mine, trembled. Her cheeks were flushed—she was sorry for me. Compassion—a feeling to which all women are prone—had caught her inexperienced heart in its clutches. Throughout the walk she was distracted and did not flirt with anyone, and that is a great sign!

We came to the gap. The ladies left their escorts, but she did not release my arm. The witticisms of the local dandies did not amuse her; the steepness of the precipice by which she stood did not frighten her, although the other ladies squealed and closed their eyes.

I did not renew our melancholy conversation on the way back. She answered my empty questions and jokes shortly and absent-mindedly.

"Have you ever loved anyone?" I asked her at last.

She looked at me steadily, shook her head, and again fell into a reverie. It was obvious that she wanted to say something but she did not know how to begin. Her bosom was heaving. These things will happen—a muslin sleeve is a poor defense, and an electric spark ran from my arm into hers.

Although every passion starts like this, we are often greatly deceived when we think that a woman loves us for our physical or mental virtues. These things prepare us, of course, and dispose us to the sacred fire; but it is always the first touch which decides the matter.

"I have been very amiable today, have I not?" the princess said to me, forcing a smile, as we were returning from the walk.

We parted.

She is displeased with herself. She is accusing herself of coldness. Oh, that is the first, the most important victory! Tomorrow she will want to compensate me. I know it all by heart—that's what's so boring.

4th June

I saw Vera a little while ago. She wore me out with her jealousy. It seems that the princess has taken it into her head to entrust the secrets of her heart to her. I must admit it's a fortunate choice!

"I know what it will lead to," Vera was telling me. "Better simply tell me now that you love her."

"But what if I don't love her?"

"Then why do you pursue and alarm her so and stir up illusions? . . . Oh, I know you so well. Listen, if you want me to believe you, come to Kislovodsk for a week. We're going there the day after tomorrow. The old princess is staying on here longer. We'll rent apartments next door to each other. We're going to live on the mezzanine of a big house near the spring. Countess Ligovskoi is downstairs, and the house next door belongs to the same landlady and hasn't been taken yet. Will you come?"

I promised—and sent away the very same day to rent the apartment.

Grushnitski called on me at six o'clock this evening and announced that his uniform would be ready tomorrow, just in time for the ball.

"At last I shall dance with her the whole evening. . . . There, I'm talking too much!" he added.

"When's the ball?"

"Tomorrow of course! Didn't you know? It's a great holiday, and the local authorities are going to organize it."

"Let's go down the boulevard."

"Not for anything in this disgusting cloak . . ."

"What, don't you like it anymore?"

I went on my own and, meeting Princess Mary, asked her for a mazurka. She seemed surprised and overjoyed.

"I thought you danced only in cases of necessity, like the last time," she said, smiling very sweetly.

She did not seem to notice Grushnitski's absence at all.

"You will be pleasantly surprised tomorrow," I told her.

"By what?"

"It's a secret. You'll find out for yourself at the ball."

I ended the evening at the old princess's. There were no visitors except for Vera and one quite ridiculous old man. I was in good spirits and made up all sorts of unusual stories. The young princess sat facing me and listened to my nonsense with such deep, intense, and even tender attention that my conscience pricked me. Where was her liveliness, her coquetry, her caprices, her arrogant bearing, the scornful smile, the distracted look?

Vera noticed all this. Her ailing face looked terribly sad. She was sitting in the shadow of the window, huddled up in a large armchair. I began to feel sorry for her.

Then I told the whole dramatic story of my rela-

tions with her and our love—concealing everything
with imaginary names, of course.

I spoke so vividly about my feelings, my turmoils
and transports, and put her conduct and character
in such a good light that, in spite of herself, she had
to forgive me my flirtation with the princess.

She got up, sat down near us, and brightened up
a good deal. It was two o'clock in the morning before we remembered that the doctor had ordered
us to bed at eleven.

5th June

Half an hour before the ball, Grushnitski reported
to me in the full splendor of an infantry uniform.
From the third button, there hung a little bronze
chain to which an eye-glass was attached. The
epaulettes, which were of incredible proportions,
were bent up to look like the wings of a small
cupid. His boots creaked. In his left hand, he was
holding brown kid gloves and a peaked cap, while
his right was constantly trying to twist his fluffy hair
into tiny curls. Complacency and, at the same time,
a certain lack of confidence were evident on his
face. His festive exterior and proud bearing would
have made me roar with laughter if that had been
consistent with my intentions. He threw the cap
and gloves onto the table and started to pull at his
coattails and adjust himself in front of the mirror. A
huge black neckerchief, wound over the highest of
stiffeners, whose wires supported his chin, protruded half an inch outside his collar. That seemed
too little for him, and he pulled it up to his ears. His
face turned very red trying to accomplish this difficult task, for the collar of the uniform was very
narrow and uncomfortable.

"They say you pursue my princess quite relentlessly these days," he said rather carelessly without looking at me.

"It's not for fools like us to drink tea," I replied, repeating a favorite saying of one of the cleverest rogues of former times, once sung by Pushkin.

"Do tell me, does the uniform fit me well? Oh, the damned Jew! It cuts under the armpits! Have you got any perfume?"

"My dear chap, what else do you want? You already smell of rose pomade."

"Never mind that. Give it to me."

He used half the bottle on his cravat, his handkerchief, and sleeves.

"Are you going to dance?" he asked.

"I don't think so."

"I'm afraid that the princess and I will have to start the mazurka. I hardly know a step . . ."

"But have you asked her for the mazurka?"

"Not yet."

"Mind that you're not forestalled."

"Really?" he said, hitting his forehead. "Goodbye . . . I'm going to wait for her by the entrance." He snatched up his cap and departed in haste. Half an hour later I too set off. The streets were dark and empty. A crowd had gathered outside the assembly rooms, or the tavern, whichever you care to call it. Its windows were bright and the evening wind carried the strains of regimental music over to me. I walked slowly; I was sad. Can it be, I thought, that my only purpose on earth is to destroy the hopes of others? Ever since I lived and entered into action, fate has somehow led me to the climax of other people's dramas, as if no one could die, no one could despair without me. I have always been the essential character of the fifth act. Involuntarily I have performed the miserable role of executioner or betrayer. What object did fate have in doing this?

Surely I am not intended to be the author of bourgeois tragedies and domestic novels or to collaborate with a supplier of short stories to the "Reader's Library," for instance . . . But how do I know? Is there any shortage of people who begin life thinking that they will end it like Alexander the Great or Lord Byron, but who remain government clerks all their lives?

I went into the hall, hid myself among a crowd of men, and began to make my observations. Grushnitski was standing beside the princess and was saying something very heatedly. She was listening to him inattentively, looking from one side to the other, her fan against her lips. She seemed impatient, and was looking around for someone. I went quietly up behind them so that I could eavesdrop on their conversation.

"You're tormenting me, Princess!" Grushnitski was saying. "You have changed terribly since I last saw you."

"You have also changed," she answered, stealing a swift derisive glance at him, which he failed to comprehend.

"I? I have changed? . . . Oh, never! You know that's impossible. He who has seen you once will always carry away your heavenly image with him."

"Stop!"

"Why don't you want to hear things now which you were pleased to listen to not long ago?"

"Because I don't like repetition," she answered with a little laugh.

"Oh, I have made a terrible mistake! Like a fool I thought that these epaulettes would at least give me the right to hope. No, it would have been better for me to remain for ever in that despicable soldier's cloak, to which, perhaps, I owed your attention."

"In fact the cloak suits you much better."

At that moment I went up to the princess and bowed. She gave a little blush and said hastily:

"Monsieur Pechorin, is it not true that the gray cloak suits Monsieur Grushnitski much better?"

"I disagree," I replied, "he looks still younger in his uniform." Grushnitski could not stand this blow. Like all boys he has pretensions to be an old man. He thinks that the deep signs of passion on his face are a substitute for the marks of age. He looked at me furiously, stamped his foot, and stalked away.

"But you admit," I told the princess, "that although he has always been quite ridiculous, not very long ago you thought he was interesting . . . in his gray cloak?"

She looked down and did not answer.

Grushnitski followed the princess about the whole evening, dancing either with her or *vis-à-vis*. He eyed her greedily, sighed, and bored her with entreaties and reproaches. By the end of the third quadrille she hated him.

"I didn't expect that of you," he said, coming up to me and taking me by the arm.

"What?"

"Are you dancing the mazurka with her?" he asked in a grave voice. "She admitted to me . . ."

"Well, what of it? Is it a secret?"

"Of course . . . I should have expected it of a hussy . . . of a coquette. But I'll be revenged!"

"Blame your cloak or your epaulettes for that, but why accuse her? Why is she guilty just because she doesn't like you anymore?"

"Why did she hold out hopes, then?"

"Why did you have hopes—I can understand wanting something or getting something, but who hopes for something?"

"You've won your bet—but not completely," he said, with a malicious smile.

The mazurka started. Grushnitski asked only the princess, and the other partners asked her every other minute. It was obviously a conspiracy against me. All the better: she wants to talk to me, and they prevent her, so she will want to twice as much.

I pressed her hand twice. The second time she pulled it away without saying a word.

"I shall sleep badly tonight," she told me when the mazurka ended.

"Grushnitski's to blame for that."

"Oh no!" and her face looked so pensive, so sad, that I promised myself that I would kiss her hand that night without fail.

People started to go. As I helped the princess into her carriage, I pressed her little hand swiftly to my lips. It was dark and no one could see.

I went back into the hall very pleased with myself.

The young people, among them Grushnitski, were having supper around a large table. Everybody stopped talking when I came in. They had obviously been talking about me. Many of them have a grudge against me since the last ball, especially the captain of dragoons, and now there seems to be no doubt that a hostile clique is being formed against me under Grushnitski's command. He has such a proud, brave air.

I am very glad; I love enemies, though not in the Christian sense. They divert me; they stir my blood. To be always on my guard, to intercept every glance and catch the significance of every word, to divine intentions and foil intrigues, to pretend to be deceived and then suddenly to overturn the whole huge labored construction of schemes and plots with a single blow—that is what I call life. Throughout supper, Grushnitski whispered and exchanged winks with the captain of dragoons.

6th June

This morning Vera left with her husband for Kislovodsk. I met their carriage as I was walking to Princess Ligovskoi's. She nodded to me. She looked reproachful.

Who is to blame? Why will she not give me a chance to be alone with her? Love is like a fire— without fuel it goes out. But perhaps jealousy will accomplish what my entreaties could not.

I stayed at the princess's for over an hour. Mary did not appear; she is ill. She was not on the boulevard this evening. The newly formed clique, armed with lorgnettes, has taken on a really menacing look. I am glad that the princess is ill. They would have done her a mischief. Grushnitski's hair is tousled and he looks despondent. He seems really distressed and his pride has been wounded. But there are people in whom even despondency is ridiculous.

Returning home, I realized that something was missing. *I had not seen her. She is ill*. Surely I have not actually fallen in love with her? How absurd!

7th June

At eleven o'clock in the morning, the hour when Princess Ligovskoi is usually sweating in the Yermolovski baths, I walked past her house. Princess Mary was sitting thoughtfully by the window. She jumped up when she saw me.

I went into the hall. There was no one about; taking advantage of the informality of local manners, I entered the drawing room unannounced.

The princess's pretty face was covered with a dull pallor. She was standing by the piano, one arm resting on the back of an armchair. The hand was trembling very slightly. I went up to her quietly and said:

"Are you annoyed with me?"

She raised a deep, languorous look to me and shook her head. Her lips wanted to say something but could not. Her eyes filled with tears. She sank into the armchair and covered her face with her hands.

"What's the matter with you?" I said, taking her hand.

"You don't respect me . . . Oh, leave me alone!"

I took a few paces toward the door. She straightened herself in the armchair and her eyes lit up.

I halted, took hold of the door handle, and said:

"Forgive me, Princess! I have behaved like an idiot . . . it won't happen again. I shall turn over a new leaf. Why should you know what's happened in my heart up till now? You will never find out, and so much the better for you. Good-bye."

As I went out I thought I heard her crying.

I wandered about the foot of Mashuk until evening, got terribly tired, and walked home, threw myself on to the bed, completely exhausted.

Werner called on me.

"Is it true," he asked, "that you are going to marry Princess Mary?"

"What?"

"The whole town says so. All my patients are full of this important news, and my patients are a crowd that know everything."

That's Grushnitski's doing, I thought.

"In order to prove to you, Doctor, that these rumors are false, I shall tell you a secret. I'm going to Kislovodsk tomorrow."

"And the princess too?"

"No, she's staying here another week."

"So you're not getting married?"

"Doctor, Doctor, look at me. Do I look like a bridegroom or anything of the sort?"

"I'm not saying that. But you know there are circumstances," he added with a sly smile, "when an honorable man is obliged to marry, and there are mammas who at least don't prevent these occurrences. So I advise you, as a friend, to be more careful. The air is very dangerous at the spa. I've seen so many marvelous young people, who deserve the best of fortunes, leaving here straight for the altar. Would you believe it, they even wanted to get me married! It was a certain local mamma, whose daughter looked very pale. I had the misfortune to tell her that the color would return after marriage. Then, with tears of thanks, she offered me her daughter's hand and all her fortune—fifty serfs, I think it was. But I replied that I wasn't so disposed."

Werner left fully convinced that he had put me on my guard.

From what he said I noticed that various nasty rumors about the princess and me had been spread about the town. It will avail Grushnitski nothing.

10th June

This is my third day in Kislovodsk. I see Vera every day at the well and while she is taking her walk. I sleep late in the mornings, then I sit down by the window and train my eye-glass on her balcony. She has been dressed long since and waits for the agreed sign. We meet as if by chance in the gardens which stretch from our houses down to the well. The invigorating mountain air has restored her strength and brought the color back to her face. No wonder Narzan is called the heroes' spring. The people who live there declare that the air of Kislovodsk inclines one to love, that all romances that have ever started at the foot of Mashuk reach their climax here. And in fact everything here breathes solitude. Everything is mysterious. The lime walks cast deep shadows as they lead down to the stream, which splashes and foams from stone to stone, cutting a path for itself through green-looking mountains. The ravines, full of mist and silence, branch off in all directions. The air is fresh and aromatic, laden with the exhalations of the high southern grass and white acacia. The cold streams which merge at the end of the valley make a continual, pleasantly soporific sound as they run friendly races with each other until at last they fall into the Podkumok. The ravine widens on this side to become a green valley. A dusty road winds over it. Every time I look at it I think I see a carriage with a rosy face looking out of its window. Many carriages have passed along that road—but not hers as yet. The suburb beyond the fort is crowded. In the evening, the lights of the assembly rooms, which are on a hill a few steps from my apartment, begin to shine through a double row of poplars. The noise and the clinking of glasses can be heard far into the night.

Nowhere is so much Kakhetin wine and mineral water drunk as here.

> But to mix these two drinks
> Is an ignorance of amateurs
> And I'm not one of them.

Every day Grushnitski and his clique carouse in the inn; he hardly acknowledges me.

He arrived only yesterday, and has already managed to quarrel with three old men who wanted to get into the bath before him. Misfortune has certainly developed his aggressive instincts.

11th June

They have come at last. I was sitting by the window when I heard the rumble of their carriage, My heart leaped. What can this be? Am I in love? I am such a foolish creature that it might be expected of me.

I dined with them. The old princess looks at me very tenderly and does not leave her daughter's side . . . which is bad! But then Vera is jealous of the princess and me. I have managed to achieve that happy state! What will a woman not do to distress her rival? I remember that someone once loved me because I loved someone else. There is nothing more paradoxical than a woman's mind. It is difficult to convince women of something; one must lead them to believe that they have convinced themselves. The chain of reasoning by which they negate their prejudices is very original. If one is to understand their dialectic, one must turn all the rules of logic upside-down. For instance, the usual form of reasoning is:

This man loves me, but I am married—therefore I ought not to love him.

The female way of arguing is:

I ought not to love him because I am married; but he loves me, therefore . . .

There are several points here. Reason never plays any part at all. As a rule the things that count are the tongue, the eyes, and, after them, the heart, if there is one.

What would happen if these notes should ever fall under a woman's eyes? "Slander!" she would cry indignantly.

Ever since poets have written and women have read them (for which they have my deepest thanks), they have been called angels so often that in their innocence they have actually come to believe it, forgetting that, for money, the same poets extolled Nero as a demigod.

I should not talk about women with such malice —I who love nothing in the world apart from them —I who have always been ready to sacrifice my

peace of mind, my ambition, my life for them. . . .
But, then, I am not trying to strip them of that
enchanted veil, transparent only to the experienced
eye, because I feel spiteful and my pride is hurt. No,
everything I say about them is but the result of

A mind that coldly notices,
A sorrowfully observing heart.

Women should wish that all men understood
them as well as I do, for I love them a hundred times
more since I stopped being afraid of them and
came to understand their little weaknesses. By the
way: the other day Werner compared women to
the enchanted forest, which Tasso talks about in
his *Jerusalem Freed.* "Only approach it," he said,
"and such terrors fly out toward you from all sides—
duty, pride, decency, common repute, jeers, contempt—that may God preserve you. You must not
heed them but go straight on, and gradually the
apparitions disappear, and a quiet bright field opens
up before you, in whose center there blooms a green
myrtle. But what misfortune awaits you if your heart
sinks at the first steps and you turn back!"

12th June

This evening was rich in events. About two miles
from Kislovodsk, in a ravine through which the
Podkumok runs, there is a rock called The Ring.
It is a natural gateway. It rises up on a high hill,
and through it the setting sun throws its last fiery
glance at the earth. A great cavalcade set off for
it to see the sun set through the little stone window.
To tell the truth, none of us was thinking about the
sun. I rode beside the princess. On the way back
we had to ford the Podkumok. Even the smallest
mountain streams are dangerous, especially because

their beds are veritable kaleidoscopes. They change from day to day with the force of current. Where there was a stone yesterday, there is a hole today. I took the princess's horse by the bridle and led it into the water, which was no more than knee-high. Carefully we began to move across at an angle against the current. It is well known that one must not look at the water when one crosses a quick-running stream, for if one does, one's head immediately starts to spin. I forgot to warn the princess about this.

We had already reached the middle where the current was swiftest when she suddenly swayed in the saddle. "I don't feel well," she said weakly. I bent swiftly over toward her, put my arm around her supple waist. "Look up," I whispered to her, "there's nothing to be afraid of. I am with you!"

She began to feel better and tried to free herself from my arm, but I clutched her soft, tender body still tighter. My cheek was almost touching hers. She was burning hot.

"What are you doing with me? Oh God!"

I paid no attention to her trembling and embarrassment, and my lips touched her soft cheek. She shuddered but said nothing. We were riding at the back so no one saw. When we reached the bank, everyone else rode off at a trot but the princess held her horse back. I stayed beside her. My silence was obviously disturbing her, but I vowed not to say a word—out of curiosity. I wanted to see how she would extricate herself from her difficult position.

"You must either despise me, or love me very much," she said at last, in a tearful voice. "You probably want a little laugh at my expense; you want to rouse my emotions and then leave me. That would be so base, so low, there can only be one supposition. . . . Oh, no! Isn't it true," she added in a soft, trusting voice, "isn't it true there's nothing about me that would prevent respect? Your boldness . . . I should, I should forgive you your boldness because I allowed . . . Answer me, say something, I want to hear your voice!" There was such feminine impatience in the last words that I could not help smiling. Fortunately, it was beginning to get dark. I did not answer.

"Aren't you going to say anything?" she continued. "Perhaps you want me to be the first to say that I love you?"

I said nothing.

"Is that what you want?" she continued, turning swiftly toward me. There was something decidedly frightening about her voice and the way she looked at me.

"Why should I?" I replied, shrugging my shoulders.

She whipped up her horse and galloped off at full speed along the narrow, dangerous road. It happened so quickly that I could hardly catch up with her, and then only when she had already joined the others. She talked and laughed all the way back. There was something feverish about her movements. She did not look at me once. Everyone noticed this unusual gaiety, and the old princess inwardly rejoiced as she watched her. But her daughter was merely having a nervous fit; she will spend a sleepless night and will cry. The thought of this gives me tremendous pleasure—there are moments when I understand the Vampire. And I am still reputed to be a thoroughly decent fellow and I try to keep up that reputation.

The ladies dismounted and went into the princess's place. I felt agitated and galloped off to the mountains to blow away the thoughts which were crowding in my head. The dewy evening smelled delightfully cool. The moon was rising from behind the dark peaks. Every step my unshod horse made reverberated dully in the silence of the ravine. I watered the horse at a fall, took one or two hungry gulps of the fresh air of the southern night, and set off on the return journey. I rode through the suburb. The lights in the windows were beginning to go out. The sentries on the fortress walls and the Cossacks in the neighboring pickets were calling out to each other in their drawling voices.

I noticed that one of the houses in the suburb, built on the edge of a gorge, was extraordinarily brightly lit. Now and again discordant chatter and shouting came from it, indicating that some officers were having a party. I dismounted and crept up to the window. A badly fitting shutter allowed me to see the revelers and eavesdrop on what they were saying. They were talking about me.

The captain of dragoons, heated with wine, was banging his fist on the table, demanding attention.

"Gentlemen," he said, "I've never heard anything like it. We must teach Pechorin a lesson! These pups from St. Petersburg always think they're the tops until they get a punch on the nose. He thinks that because he always wears clean gloves and polished boots he's the only one in the world!"

"And what a supercilious smile he's got! But I'm convinced he's a coward, all the same—yes, a coward!"

"I think so too," said Grushnitski. "He likes to pass things off as a joke. I said certain things to him once which would have made another man cut me down on the spot, but Pechorin just turned it into a joke. Of course, I didn't challenge him because it was his affair; and I didn't want to get mixed up in . . ."

"Grushnitski hates him because he took the princess away from him," someone said.

"What will you think of next? It's true I did pay some attention to the princess, but I stopped immediately, because I didn't want to get married, and I don't think it's right to compromise a girl."

"Yes, I assure you he's a first-class coward, that is, Pechorin, not Grushnitski. Grushnitski's a great chap and my true friend too." This was the captain of dragoons again. "Gentlemen, does anyone here stand up for him? No one? So much the better! Do you want to test his courage? It'll amuse you."

"We'd like to. But how?"

"Well, now, listen to me. Grushnitski is particularly annoyed with him, so he should play the leading part. He'll take exception to some small thing or other and challenge Pechorin to a duel. Wait now, this is the point. . . . He'll challenge him to a duel: very well then! Everything about it—the challenge, the preparations, the conditions—will be as serious and frightening as possible. I'll see to that. I shall be your second, my poor friend. Very well then. But here's the catch: We won't load the pistols. I'll vouch that Pechorin funks it—I'll fix it at six paces, damn it! Do you agree, gentlemen?"

"It's a marvelous idea. Agreed! Why on earth not?" Such comments sounded on all sides.

"What about you, Grushnitski?"

I trembled as I waited for Grushnitski's answer. A cold hatred crept over me at the thought that if it were not for this chance, these idiots might have made a fool of me. If Grushnitski did not agree, I would throw myself around his neck. But, after a few moments' silence he rose from his chair, stretched out his hand to the captain and said very pompously, "Very well, I agree!"

F

The elation of everyone in that honorable company is difficult to describe.

I went home, disturbed by two different emotions. The first was sorrow. Why do they all hate me? I thought. Why? Have I offended anybody? No. Surely I am not one of those people who arouse ill will on sight? At the same time I felt a poisonous malignity creep over me. Take care, Mister Grushnitski, I said, as I walked up and down my room. You don't play games like that with me. You may pay dearly for the approval of your silly friends. I'm not a toy for you to play with . . .

I did not sleep all night. By morning I looked as yellow as a wild orange.

I met the princess at the well this morning.

"Are you ill?" she said looking at me intently.

"I didn't sleep all night."

"Nor did I . . . I blame you . . . unjustly perhaps? But explain yourself—I can forgive you everything."

"Everything?"

"Everything . . . but you must tell the truth . . . and quickly. . . . You see, I have thought a great deal and tried to explain, to excuse your conduct. Perhaps you are afraid that my parents will raise obstacles . . . don't worry about that. When they find out . . . (her voice started to tremble) I'll talk them around. Or perhaps it's your position. But you must understand that I can sacrifice everything for the man I love. Oh, answer me quickly, have pity. . . . You don't despise me, do you?"

She caught hold of my hand.

The old princess was walking in front of us with Vera's husband and saw nothing. But the invalids who were walking about—the most inquisitive scandalmongers—they could see us, and I quickly freed my hand from her passionate grasp.

"I'll tell you the whole truth," I answered the

princess, "I won't excuse or explain my conduct. I don't love you."

The color faded from her lips.

"Leave me alone," she said, barely audibly.

I shrugged my shoulders, turned, and walked away.

14th June

Sometimes I despise myself . . . perhaps that is why I despise other people. I have become incapable of generosity; I am afraid of seeming ridiculous to myself. Another man in my place would have offered the princess *son coeur et sa fortune,* but the word "marriage" has a magic power over me. However passionately I love a woman, she has only to make me feel that I ought to marry her and goodbye to love! My heart turns to stone, and nothing will warm it again. I am prepared to sacrifice anything but that. Twenty times in my life I have even staked my honor on a card . . . but I will not sell my freedom. Why do I treasure it so much? What does it mean to me? What am I preparing myself for? What do I expect of the future? To tell the truth, exactly nothing. It is a kind of unreasonable fear, an inherent sense of foreboding. But then there are people who have an unreasonable fear of spiders, cockroaches, mice. Shall I confess? When I was still a child, an old woman told my fortune to my mother. She prophesied that I should *die by the hand of an evil woman*. It made a great impression on me at the time, and an uncontrollable aversion to marriage was born in me. Anyway something tells me that this prophecy will come true but at least I shall try to postpone it for as long as I can.

15th June

The conjuror Apfelbaum arrived here yesterday.

A large poster appeared on the doors of the restaurant informing the esteemed public that the most celebrated and amazing conjuror, acrobat, alchemist, and illusionist would have the honor to give a magnificent exhibition this day at eight o'clock in the evening in the hall of the Hall of Noble Assembly (otherwise—the assembly rooms); tickets two rubles fifty kopecks each.

Everybody is going to see the amazing conjuror. Even Princess Ligovskoi has bought herself a ticket, although her daughter is ill.

Just now, after dinner, I was walking past Vera's window. She was sitting alone on the balcony. A note fell at my feet:

> Come up to me at ten o'clock this evening by the main staircase. My husband has gone to Pyatigorsk and will not return until tomorrow morning. My servants and maids will be out, I gave them all tickets, and the princess's servants too. I expect you. Do not fail to come.

Ah, I thought, at last it's turned out my way!

At eight o'clock I went to watch the conjuror. The audience assembled toward nine, and the performance commenced. I noticed Vera's and the princess's servants and maids in the back rows. Absolutely everyone was there. Grushnitski was sitting in the front row with an eye-glass. The conjuror turned to him every time he needed a handkerchief, a watch, a ring, and so forth.

Grushnitski has not acknowledged me for some time, but he looked at me rather insolently once or twice this evening. He will remember all this when we come to settle our account.

Just before ten I got up and left.

Outside it was dark enough to hurt your eyes.

Cold, heavy clouds lay on the peaks of the surrounding mountains. Only occasionally did the dying wind sound in the tops of the poplars which surround the assembly rooms. A crowd was milling around the windows. I walked down the hill and, turning in at the gateway, quickened my pace. Suddenly I thought someone was following me. I stopped and looked around. I could make nothing out in the dark, but to be on the safe side, I walked right around the house as if I were having a stroll. As I passed the princess's window I heard steps behind me again. A man wrapped in a cloak ran past me. That alarmed me, but nevertheless I crept up to the porch and ran hurriedly up the dark staircase. A door opened; a tiny hand caught hold of my arm.

"No one saw you?" Vera whispered, pressing close to me.

"No one!"

"Now do you believe that I love you? Oh, I have hesitated and tormented myself for so long . . . but you do what you like with me."

Her heart was beating fiercely, her hands were as cold as ice. Then the reproaches, the jealousy, the complaints. She demanded that I admit everything, and said she would resign herself to my faithlessness because she only wanted my happiness. I did not altogether believe it, but I quietened her with vows, promises, and so on.

"So you're not going to marry Mary! You don't love her! . . . But she thinks . . . you know, she dotes on you, poor thing!"

.   .   .   .

About two o'clock in the morning I opened the window and, tying two shawls together and hold-

ing onto a pillar, lowered myself from Vera's balcony to the one beneath. A fire was still burning in
the princess's room. Something drew me toward her
window. The curtains were not quite drawn together, and I was able to cast an inquisitive glance
into the room. Mary was sitting on the bed, her arms
crossed over her knees. Her thick hair was drawn
up under a lace-edged nightcap, and a large crim-
son scarf covered her small white shoulders. Her tiny
feet were hidden in colorful Persian slippers. She
was sitting quite still—her head sunk on her breast.
A book lay open on the little table in front of her,
but her eyes, motionless and full of an unutterable
sorrow, seemed to run over the same page a hundred times. Her thoughts were far away.

At that moment someone moved behind a bush.
I jumped from the balcony onto the turf. An un-
seen hand took hold of me by the shoulder.

"Aha!" said a coarse voice, "caught you! So you
visit princesses at night."

"Hold him tighter!" called out someone else, rushing out from behind the corner.

It was Grushnitski and the captain of dragoons.

I punched the latter on the head, knocking him
off his feet, and threw myself into the bushes. I
knew every path in the garden, which covered the
slope opposite our houses.

"Thieves! Guards!" they called. There was a rifle
shot, and a smoking piece of wadding fell almost at
my feet.

A minute later I was in my room; I undressed and
went to bed. My manservant had hardly locked the
door when Grushnitski and the captain began to
knock on it.

"Pechorin! Are you asleep? Are you here?" cried
the captain.

"I'm sleeping," I replied with annoyance.

"Get up! Thieves . . . Circassians . . ."

"I've got a cold in the head," I replied, "and don't want it to get worse."

They went away. I should not have answered them—they would have spent another hour looking for me in the garden. Meanwhile the alarm had been raised with a vengeance. Cossacks rode down from the fort. There was a tremendous stir. People were looking for Circassians in every bush—and of course they found nothing. However I daresay that many people are still firmly convinced that if the garrison had shown more courage and speed, at least a couple of dozen plunderers would have been found in the place.

16th June

This morning at the well there was nothing but chatter about the night attack of the Circassians. Having drunk the proper number of glasses of Narzan water and walked about a dozen times up and down the long avenue of limes, I met Vera's husband, who had only just arrived from Pyatigorsk. He took me by the arm, and we went into the assembly rooms for breakfast. He was terribly worried arout his wife. "She was so frightened last night!" he said. "Of course it had to happen just when I was away!" We sat down to breakfast near a door leading to a corner room, where there were ten or so young people, including Grushnitski. Again fate gave me the chance to eavesdrop on a conversation which was to decide his destiny. He did not see me, and so I could not suspect that I was intended to hear. But that only increased his guilt in my eyes.

"It wasn't really Circassians?" someone said. "Did anyone see them?"

"I'll tell you the whole truth," replied Grushnitski,

"but please don't give me away. This is what happened: last night a certain man, whom I will not name, came and told me that at ten o'clock in the evening he saw someone creeping into the Ligovskois' house. I must explain that the old princess was here, but the young princess was at home. So he and I took up positions near the windows in order to ambush the lucky man."

I must admit I was frightened, even though my companion was very occupied with his breakfast. He might hear some rather unpleasant things if only Grushnitski had guessed the truth. But, blinded by jealousy, he did not suspect her.

"So you see," continued Grushnitski, "we went off there, taking a musket loaded with a blank cartridge with us just to give him a fright. We waited in the garden until two o'clock. At last he appeared—God knows where from, but not from the window, because it wasn't opened. He must have come through the glass door behind the column. At last, then, we saw someone coming down from the balcony . . . what a Princess for you, eh? Well, I must say these Moscow ladies are something! What can you believe after that? We tried to catch him, but he broke away and darted into the bushes like a hare. Then I shot at him." A buzz of incredulity sounded around Grushnitski.

"You don't believe it?" he continued. "I give you my word of honor as a gentleman that it's the absolute truth, and if you like, I'll name the gentleman to prove it."

"Tell us, tell us who he is," they all clamored.

"Pechorin," Grushnitski replied.

At that moment he raised his eyes—I was standing in the doorway opposite him. He turned very red. I went up to him and, slowly and distinctly, said:

"I'm sorry that I came in after you had given your word of honor in support of the most disgusting slander. My presence would have saved you from perjuring yourself further."

Grushnitski jumped up and started to make a fuss.

"I ask you," I continued in the same tone, "I ask you to repudiate this instant what you said. You know very well it's an invention, and I don't think a woman's indifference to your shining qualities deserves such a terrible revenge. Think carefully. If you persist in this opinion, you'll lose the right to be called an honorable man and you'll risk your life."

Grushnitski stood facing me with his eyes downcast in a state of great agitation. But the struggle between conscience and pride was not prolonged. The captain of dragoons, who was sitting next to him, jogged him with his elbow; he started and answered me briskly without raising his eyes:

"My dear sir, when I say something, I think it, and am prepared to repeat it. . . . Your threats do not frighten me, and I am prepared for anything."

"You've already shown that," I answered him coldly and, taking the captain of dragoons by the arm, walked out of the room.

"What do you want?" asked the captain.

"You're Grushnitski's friend—so presumably you will act as his second?"

The captain bowed very gravely.

"You are right," he replied, "I'm even obliged to be his second, because the insult aimed at him touches me as well. I was with him last night," he added, straightening his round shoulders.

"Oh! So it was your head I punched so hard?" He turned yellow and then dark blue. The malice, hidden until now, showed on his face.

"I shall have the honor to send my second to you

today," I added, bowing very politely and pretending not to notice his rage.

I met Vera's husband at the entrance to the restaurant. He must have been waiting for me.

He took hold of my hand with a spirit akin to rapture.

"What an honorable young man!" he said with tears in his eyes: "I heard everything. What a rascal! What an ungrateful fellow! To think of accepting them into a respectable house after this! Thank God I have no daughters. But she you risk your life for will reward you. You may rest assured that I shall be discreet until the proper moment, until the time comes," he continued. "I too was young and served in the army. I know one mustn't interfere in affairs like this. Good-bye."

Poor man! He rejoices that he has no daughters . . .

I went straight to Werner's and found him at home. I told him everything—about my relationships with Vera and the princess, and the conversation from which I learned that these gentlemen intended to make a fool of me by making me fight a duel with blank cartridges. But now things had gone beyond a joke: presumably they had not expected a development like this.

The doctor agreed to be my second. I gave him a few instructions about the conditions of the duel. He should insist that it take place as secretly as possible, for although I am always ready to die, I am not at all disposed to spoil forever my future in this world.

After this I went home. An hour later the doctor returned from his expedition.

"There really is a conspiracy against you," he said. "I found the captain of dragoons and another gentleman, whose name I can't remember, at

Grushnitski's. I stopped in the hall for a moment to take off my galoshes. They were arguing and making an awful din . . . 'I won't agree to that for anything!' Grushnitski was saying, 'He insulted me in public. It was quite another matter before.' 'What are you worried about?' replied the captain. 'I'll take the responsibility for everything. I've acted as second in five duels and I know how to manage it. I've thought of everything. Just don't obstruct me, for goodness' sake. There's nothing wrong in giving him a bit of a fright. And why expose yourself to danger if you can avoid it?' At that moment I went in. They suddenly became silent. Our negotiations were quite lengthy. At last we agreed on this: there's a lonely gorge three miles from here. They'll ride out there at four o'clock tomorrow morning; we'll leave half an hour after them. The duel will be fought at six paces—Grushnitski demanded that himself. A death will be blamed on the Circassians. Now, my suspicions are these: they, that is the seconds, have made a slight change in their previous plan and now want to put a bullet only in Grushnitski's pistol. It's more like murder, but cunning is permissible in war, especially in Asiatic war. However, Grushnitski seems to be rather more honorable than his comrades. What do you think? Shall we show them that we know what they're up to?"

"Not for anything in the world, Doctor! Don't worry, I won't sacrifice myself to them."

"What do you intend to do?"

"That's my secret."

"Mind they don't catch you out . . . it's only six paces, you know!"

"Doctor, I shall expect you tomorrow morning at four o'clock. The horse will be ready. . . . Good-bye."

I stayed at home, shut up in my room, until

evening. A lackey came to invite me to the princess's
—I bade him say I was ill.

Two o'clock in the morning . . . I can't sleep . . .
but I must get to sleep if my hand is not to shake
tomorrow. Anyway, it is difficult to miss at six
paces. Oh, Mister Grushnitski! Your trickery will
avail you nothing. . . . the roles shall be changed. . . .
Now it will be my turn to look for signs of secret
fear on your pale face. Why did you yourself pro-
pose these deadly six paces? You think that I shall
offer you my head without an argument, but we
shall throw lots! and then . . . then . . . what if he
has the luck, what if my stars betray me at last?
And it could happen—they have served my whims
faithfully for so long, and there is no more constancy
in heaven than upon earth.

What of it? If I die, I die. It will be no great loss
to the world, and I am thoroughly bored with life. I
am like a man yawning at a ball; the only reason he
does not go home to bed is that his carriage has not
arrived yet. But the carriage awaits . . . so farewell!

As I turn the recollections of my past over in my
mind, I cannot help asking myself why I lived. What
was the object of my being born? There must have
been one, and I must have been intended for great
things because I feel unbounded powers in me. But
I did not discover where that destiny lay. I was lured
away by enticements of empty and unrewarding passions. I emerged from their furnace as hard and cold
as iron. But the heat of noble aspirations—the
finest bloom of life—had gone forever. How many
times since then have I played the role of an ax in
the hands of fate! I have fallen on the head of
doomed victims like an instrument of punishment,
often without malice and always without pity. My
love has brought happiness to no one, because I

never sacrificed anything for those I loved. I loved
for my own sake, for my own pleasure; I was merely
satisfying the strange need of my heart, hungrily
devouring their feelings, their tenderness, their joys
and sufferings—and I could never be sated. I have
been like a man who, exhausted by hunger, falls
asleep from weakness and sees a sumptuous meal
and sparkling wine in front of him. He devours the
heavenly gifts of the inspiration with delight, and he
feels better, but as soon as he wakes up—the dream
disappears and he is left with his hunger and despair
redoubled!

Perhaps I shall die tomorrow! And not a single
person will remain in the world who understood me
completely. Some think me worse, others better, than
I really am. Some will say: he was a good, a decent
chap; others: he was a rogue. And both will be
wrong. Is it worthwhile living after this? But you
still live on out of curiosity. You wait for something
new. . . . It is funny and annoying!

I have been six weeks now in the fortress of I—.
Maxim has gone out hunting, and I am alone. I am
sitting by the window. Gray clouds have covered
the mountains right down to their feet; the sun looks
like a yellow spot through the mist. It is cold; the
wind is howling and the shutters are banging. . . .
I feel so bored! I shall continue my journal which
was interrupted by so many strange happenings.

I am reading through the last page: it is funny! I
thought I was going to die, but that was impossible
—I still have not drained the cup of suffering, and
now I feel that I shall live even longer.

How clearly and sharply everything that has
happened has been etched in my memory! Time
has not washed away a single line or tint!

I remember that I did not sleep a minute the night

before the duel nor could I write for long. I was overcome by a mysterious excitement. For an hour I walked about the room. Afterward I sat down and opened a novel by Walter Scott, which was lying on the table nearby. It was *Old Mortality*. I found it an effort to read at first, but then I forgot myself, and the magic of the story carried me away . . . surely the Scottish bard must be rewarded in the other world for every moment of consolation his book gives? . . .

Dawn came at last. My nerves were calmed. I looked in the mirror. My face was covered with pallor and bore the traces of tormenting insomnia. But the eyes, though surrounded by brown shadows, blazed proudly and implacably. I was pleased with myself.

I ordered the horses to be saddled, got dressed, and ran down to the bathhouse. I felt my physical and mental powers revive as I sank into the cold Narzan water. I came out of the bath as fresh and braced as if I were off to a ball. After this you can say that the mind does not depend on the body!

I returned to find the doctor in my rooms. He was wearing gray riding breeches, a quilted jacket, and a Circassian cap. I started to roar with laughter at the sight of that little figure beneath an immense shaggy hat. His face is never bellicose, and this time it was even longer than usual.

"Why do you look so sad, Doctor?" I asked him. "Haven't you seen people into the next world a hundred times with the greatest indifference? Imagine I've got an inflammation of the spleen. I might recover, or on the other hand I might die— either would be in the order of things. Try to see me as a patient with a desperate illness which you still can't diagnose—and then your curiosity will be stirred in the highest degree. You may now make a few important physiological observations on me. Isn't the expectation of violent death a real illness?"

This idea amazed the doctor, and he recovered his spirits.

We mounted. Werner clutched at the reins with both hands, and we set off. In a moment we had ridden through the suburb, past the fort, and into the pass, where the road ran. It was partly overgrown with high grass and crossed every now and then by a boisterous stream which had to be forded, to the considerable despair of the doctor, whose horse stopped still in the water every time.

I cannot remember a brighter and fresher morning. The sun had hardly appeared from behind the greenish peaks, and the warmth of its rays merging with the dying coolness of the night gave everything a kind of sweet, languorous feeling. The joyous ray of the young day had not yet penetrated the ravine; it was only gilding the tops of the cliffs, which towered over us on both sides. Leafy bushes growing in their deep clefts showered a silvery rain on us at the least breath of wind. I remember that I loved nature more then than at any time before. How curiously I looked at every drop of dew which hung on a broad vine leaf, and reflected millions of iridescent points of light. How hungrily my eyes tried to peer into the smoky distance! Here the trail became narrower and narrower, the cliffs still more blue and frightening, till, at last, they seemed to come down in an impenetrable wall. We rode in silence.

"Have you made your will?" Werner asked suddenly.

"No."

"What will happen if you're killed?"

"The heirs will find out for themselves."

"Surely you must have a friend to whom you'd like to send your last wish?"

I shook my head.

"Surely there must be a woman in the world to whom you'd like to leave something to be remembered by?"

"Doctor," I answered him, "do you want me to open my heart to you? You see, I've passed the time of life when people die uttering the name of their loved one and bequeathing a friend a lock of pomaded or unpomaded hair. When I think about near and probable death, I think only of me: other people don't do this. Friends who'll forget me tomorrow—or worse, ascribe God knows what cock and bull stories to me; women who'll laugh at me while they are embracing another man, so as not to make him jealous of the deceased—the devil take the lot of them! I have acquired a few ideas from the storm of life—but not one feeling. I've lived with my head rather than my heart for a long time now. I weigh and analyze my own emotions and actions with strict attention but without partiality. There are two men in me: one lives in the full sense of the word, the other considers and judges him. In an hour's time the first will probably say good-bye to you and the world forever, but the second . . . the second? Look there, Doctor! Do you see three figures standing out on that cliff over to the right? They must be our adversaries."

We broke into a trot.

Three horses were tethered in the bushes at the foot of the cliff. We tied up ours there too and climbed up a narrow path to the place where Grushnitski was waiting for us. With him were the captain of dragoons and his other second, who was called Ivan Ignatyevich. I never heard his surname.

"We've been waiting for you a long time," said the dragoons captain with a sarcastic smile.

I took out my watch and showed it to him.

He apologized, saying that his watch was fast.

An embarrassing silence lasted several minutes. At last the doctor interrupted it, turning to Grushnitski.

"It seems to me," he said, " that since you have both shown a readiness to fight and by doing so have done what honor demands, you may be able, gentlemen, to clear up the misunderstanding and end the matter to your mutual satisfaction."

"I am ready," I said.

The captain winked at Grushnitski, and the latter, thinking that I was funking it, adopted a proud look, although until that moment he had looked as white as a sheet. For the first time since we arrived he looked straight at me, but there was a certain uneasiness in his glance which indicated an inner struggle.

"Explain your conditions," he said, "you may be sure that everything I can do for you . . ."

"These are my conditions: you will now repudiate your slander and will ask my forgiveness."

"My dear sir, I'm surprised. How dare you make such proposals?"

"What can I suggest to you apart from that?"

"We shall fight."

I shrugged my shoulders.

"As you like. But you must realize that one of us will be killed for certain."

"I hope it will be you."

"But I am convinced of the contrary . . ."

He was taken aback; he blushed, then gave a forced laugh.

The captain took him by the arm and led him aside. They whispered to each other for a long time. I was in quite a calm state of mind, but all this was beginning to get on my nerves.

The doctor came up to me.

"Listen to me," he said, with obvious concern, "you seem to have forgotten about their plot. I don't know how to load a pistol, but in this case . . . You're a strange man! Tell them you know what they intend to do and they won't dare. . . . What a business to shoot you down like a bird!"

"Don't be alarmed, Doctor, be patient. . . . I'll handle things so that they'll get no advantage. Let them whisper."

"Gentlemen, this is getting tedious!" I told them loudly, "If we're going to fight, we're going to fight; you had plenty of time to talk yesterday."

"We're ready," replied the captain. "Take your places gentlemen! Doctor, be so good as to measure out six paces."

"Take your places," repeated Ivan Ignatyevich in a squeaky voice.

"One moment, please," I said, "there's one more condition. Since we're going to fight to the death, we must do everything possible to keep this a secret so that our seconds are not held responsible. Do you agree?"

"We agree completely."

"Well, then, I have thought of this: you see the little space at the top of that sheer cliff over there to the right? It's about two hundred feet, if not more, from there to the bottom, and there are sharp rocks underneath. Each of us will stand at the very edge of the space—that way even a light wound will be fatal. That should be consistent with your wishes for you yourself stipulated six paces. Whoever is wounded will fall down and be smashed to pieces for certain. The doctor will extract the bullet, and then it will be very easy to ascribe the sudden death to an unlucky fall. We'll throw lots for who'll be the first to fire. I inform you in conclusion that failing these conditions, I shall not fight."

"Very well, then," said the captain, looking expressively at Grushnitski, who nodded his head as a sign of agreement. His face was changing every instant. I had put him in a difficult position. Fighting a duel under normal conditions he could shoot me in the leg, wound me lightly, and thus satisfy his revenge without overburdening his conscience. But now he had to fire into the air, or either make himself a murderer or eventually abandon his underhanded scheme and face danger on equal terms with me. I would not have liked to be in his shoes at that moment. He called the captain aside and began to say something to him with great urgency. I saw that his lips were blue and trembling. But the captain turned away from him with a contemptuous smile. "You're a fool!" he told Grushnitski quite loudly. "You don't understand anything! Let's start, gentlemen!"

A narrow path led up to the incline, between bushes. The precarious steps of this natural staircase consisted of pieces of rock. We started to scramble up holding onto the bushes for support. Grushnitski went first, followed by his seconds and the doctor, and I brought up the rear.

"You amaze me," said the doctor, taking a firm hold of my hand. "Let me feel your pulse. Aha! feverish! But there's nothing unusual about your face . . . except your eyes are sparkling more brightly."

Suddenly small stones rolled down under our feet. What was that? Grushnitski had stumbled; a bough he was holding onto had broken and he would have fallen down on his back if his seconds had not held him up.

"Be careful," I called out to him, "don't fall too soon; it's a bad omen. Remember Julius Caesar!"

At last we reached the top of the overhanging cliff. The ground was covered with fine sand as if expressly for a duel. The mountaintops clustered like a countless herd, losing themselves in the golden mists of morning. To the south, Elborus rose up in a white mass, the main link in the chain of icy peaks. Fibrous clouds coming over from the east were beginning to filter between them. I walked up to the edge and looked down. I felt almost giddy. It looked as dark and as cold as the grave down there. Mossy, teethlike rocks, scattered about by storms and time, were waiting for their prey.

The space on which we had to fight was an almost equilateral triangle. Six paces were measured out from the projecting corner and it was decided that the one who had to face the other's fire first, would stand at the very tip, with his back to the precipice. If he should not be killed, the opponents would change places.

I was determined to let Grushnitski have every advantage. I wanted to test him; a generous spark might be lit in his heart, and then everything would be settled for the best. But pride and weakness of character had to triumph. I wanted to give myself every right to have no mercy on him, if fate spared me. Who has not made such bargains with his conscience?

"Throw the coin, Doctor," said the captain.

The doctor took a silver piece out of his pocket and threw it up.

"Tails!" called out Grushnitski promptly, like a man suddenly aroused by a friendly jolt.

"Heads!" said I.

The coin spun and fell with a ring. Everyone rushed toward it.

"You're lucky," I told Grushnitski, "you have the first turn. But remember that if you don't kill me, I won't miss—I give you my word of honor."

He turned red; he was ashamed to kill an unarmed man. I watched him closely; for a moment I thought that he would throw himself at my feet, begging forgiveness, but how could he confess to such an ignoble plan? He had one course left—to fire into the air; I was sure that he would fire into the air! Only one thing could stop him doing that: the thought that I would demand another duel.

"The time's come!" the doctor whispered to me, pulling at my sleeve. "Everything's lost if you don't say now that we know their intentions. Look, he's already loading . . . if you won't say anything, then I will myself . . ."

"Not for anything in the world, Doctor," I replied, holding him back by his arm, "you'll spoil everything. You gave me your word you wouldn't interfere. . . . What concern is it of yours? Perhaps I want to be killed."

He looked at me with surprise.

"Oh, that's another matter! . . . But don't complain about me in the next world."

Meanwhile the captain had loaded his pistols, and gave one to Grushnitski, whispering something to him with a smile. The other he gave to me.

I stood at the corner of the triangle, bracing my left foot firmly against a stone, and bent forward slightly, so as not to fall back if I were lightly wounded.

Grushnitski stood facing me, and at a given signal he began to raise the pistol. His knees were shaking. He was aiming straight at my forehead.

I started to boil up with an inexplicable fury.

Suddenly he lowered the muzzle of the pistol and, white as a sheet, turned to his second.

"I can't," he said dully.

"Coward!" answered the captain.

A shot rang out. The bullet scratched my knee. Involuntarily I took several paces forward, so as to get away from the edge as quickly as I could.

"Well, brother Grushnitski, I'm sorry you missed," said the captain. "Now it's your turn. Take your place! But embrace me first—we won't see each other again." They embraced. The captain could hardly stop himself from laughing. "Don't be afraid," he added, glancing slyly at Grushnitski; "nothing has any significance in the world. Nature's a simpleton, fate is a goose, and life is worth but a brass farthing."

After this tragic phrase, pronounced with a proper degree of gravity, he took up his position. Ivan Ignatyevich also embraced Grushnitski with tears, and at last he remained there, alone, facing me. I am still trying to explain to myself what the feeling was that welled up inside me at that moment. It was anger at my pride being insulted, and malevolence, and contempt born at the thought that this man, who was looking at me now with such self-assurance, with such calm insolence, had tried to kill me like a dog two minutes before, without exposing himself to any danger at all. For if the wound in my leg had been any worse, I would certainly have fallen from the cliff.

I looked intently at his face for several moments, trying to find even the slightest trace of remorse. But it seemed to me that he was suppressing a smile.

"I advise you to pray to God before you die," I said.

"Don't concern yourself with my soul any more than you do with your own. I have only one request to make: shoot quickly."

"So you won't withdraw your slander? You won't

apologize? Think carefully—doesn't your conscience worry you at all?"

"Mister Pechorin," the captain cried, "allow me to point out that you're not here to hear confession. Let's get it over with. Someone might ride through the pass and see us."

"Very well. Doctor, come here."

The doctor walked up to me. Poor doctor! He looked paler than Grushnitski had ten minutes before.

I intentionally pronounced the following words as they pronounce sentence of death—loudly, distinctly, and with deliberation:

"Doctor, these gentlemen, in their haste, probably, forgot to place a bullet in my pistol. I ask you to load it again—and properly!"

"That's impossible," cried the captain, "impossible! I loaded both pistols. Perhaps the bullet fell out of yours. . . . It's not my fault! And you have no right to reload . . . no right at all . . . it's quite against the rules. I won't allow it."

"Very well!" I told the captain. "If that's the case, then I shall fight a duel with you under the same conditions."

He stopped short.

Grushnitski was standing with his head sunk on his breast. He was miserably embarrassed.

"Let them!" he said at last to the captain, who was trying to tear the pistol out of the doctor's hands. "You know perfectly well that they're right."

The captain made various signs to him in vain. Grushnitski did not even want to look.

Meanwhile the doctor loaded the pistol and gave it to me.

When he saw this, the captain spat and stamped his foot.

"You're a fool, my friend," he said, "a simple

idiot! You have relied on me for everything, so you should listen to me now. It serves you right! Get yourself swatted like a fly . . ." He turned aside and, as he walked away, muttered: "And it's quite against the rules anyway."

"Grushnitski," I said, "there's still time. Withdraw your slander, and I shall forgive you everything. You haven't succeeded in making a fool of me, and my pride is satisfied. Remember, we were friends once."

His face blazed up, his eyes flashed.

"Shoot!" he replied. "I despise myself, but I hate you. If you don't kill me, I'll lie in wait for you one night and cut your throat. There's no room for the two of us on this earth."

I fired.

When the smoke dispersed, Grushnitski was no longer there. A light cloud of dust hung above the edge of the precipice.

They all screamed at the same time.

"*Finita la commedia!*" I said to the doctor.

He did not reply and turned away in horror.

I shrugged my shoulders and took my leave of Grushnitski's seconds. On my way down along the path, I caught sight of Grushnitski's bloody corpse between the clefts in the rocks. I closed my eyes involuntarily.

I untied the horse and rode home slowly. My heart felt like a stone. The sun seemed dull; its rays gave me no warmth.

I turned off to the right down a ravine, instead of riding into the suburb. The sight of man would have been oppressive to me: I wanted to be alone. I dropped the reins, hung my head, and rode for a long time. At last I found myself in a place I did not know at all. I turned the horse around and started to look for the road. The sun was already setting when I rode, exhausted and on an exhausted horse, into Kislovodsk.

My valet told me that Werner had called and gave me two notes, one from him, the other from Vera.

I opened the first one. This is the gist of it:

Everything has been done as well as it could be. The body has been brought in disfigured, the bullet has been extracted from the chest. Everyone is satisfied that the cause of his death was an unfortunate accident. Only the commandant, who probably knows about your quarrel, shook his head, but he did not say anything. There is no evidence at all against you and you may sleep in peace . . . if you can . . . Goodbye.

I could not bring myself to open the second note for a long time. What could she write to me? I was oppressed with a heavy sense of foreboding.

Here it is, the letter whose every word is stamped indelibly on my memory:

I am writing to you in the complete certainty that we shall not see each other again. When we parted a few years ago, I thought the same, but heaven was pleased to test me again. I could not stand this test; my weak heart yielded again to the familiar voice. You do not despise me for that, do you? This letter will be both a farewell and a confession. I am bound to tell you everything that has mounted up inside me ever since I first loved you. I shall not begin to accuse you—you behaved toward me as any other man would have done: you loved me as a possession, as a source of pleasure, excitement, and misery, without which life would be boring and monotonous. I understood that from the beginning. But you were unhappy, and I sacrificed myself, hoping that one day you would appreciate my sacrifice, that one day you would understand my deep, tender, selfless love for you. Much time has passed since then. I penetrated all the secrets of your heart and became convinced that it was a vain hope. It was bitter for me! But my love had become entwined with my soul: it darkened, but the flame did not go out.

We are parting forever. But you may rest assured that I shall never love another—my heart has spent all its treasures, all its tears and hopes on you. One who has loved you once cannot look at other men without a certain disdain, not because you are better than they—oh, no! But there is some singular quality in your nature, something particular to you, something proud and mysterious. Whatever you say, your voice has an irresistible power; no one else tries so hard to be loved; in no one is evil so attractive; no other glance promises so much bliss; no one knows better how to use his advantages and no one can be as unhappy as you, for no one tries so hard to convince himself of the contrary.

I should explain the cause of my hurried departure. It will seem trivial to you because it only affects me.

My husband came into me this morning and talked about your altercation with Grushnitski. Obviously, my face must have changed a lot, because he looked me long and keenly in the eye. I almost fell senseless at the thought of your having to fight today and that I was the cause. I felt I was going out of my mind. But now I can think clearly, I am sure that you will stay alive. It is impossible that you should die without me, impossible! My husband walked about the room for a long time. I do not know what he said to me, I do not remember what I said in reply. I must have told him that I love you. I only remember that at the end of our conversation he insulted me and used a terrible word, and then he went out. I heard him ordering the carriage to be made ready. I have been sitting by the window now for three hours waiting for you to return. But you are alive, you must not die. The carriage is almost ready. . . . Farewell,

farewell. . . . I am finished, but what does it matter? If I could be sure that you would always remember me—I do not say love—no, just remember. . . . Farewell. They are coming. I must hide the letter . . .

You do not love Mary, do you? You will not marry her? Listen, you should offer me that sacrifice—I have lost everything in the world for you!

I ran out onto the porch like a madman, jumped on my Circassian horse, which was being led through the yard, and galloped off along the road to Pyatigorsk. I spurred the tired horse on without mercy, and foaming and snorting it whirled me along the stony road.

The sun was already hidden behind a black cloud, which rested on the chain of mountains to the south. It was getting dark and dank in the pass. The Podkumok roared dully and monotonously as it threaded its way among the rocks. I rode on, panting with impatience. The thought of not finding her in Pyatigorsk was hitting me in the heart like a hammer. One minute, one minute more in which to see her, say good-bye, press her hand. . . . I prayed, cursed, cried, laughed . . . no, no word can convey my alarm, my despair! Vera became dearer to me than anything in the world, and the possibility of losing her forever—dearer than life, honor, happiness. God knows what strange, what insane plans were swarming in my head. And all the time I still rode on, driving the horse without mercy. Suddenly I noticed that my horse was breathing more heavily. It stumbled once or twice on even ground. It was still three and a half miles from Yessentukov, the Cossack station where I could mount another horse.

All would have been saved had my horse's strength lasted another ten minutes. But, suddenly, on a sharp upward bend as we were emerging from the mountains, it fell abruptly to the ground. I jumped off quickly, tried to get it to its feet, pulled at the reins, but it was useless. A barely audible moan broke through its clenched teeth. It died within a few moments; I was alone on the steppe, my last hope gone. I tried walking, but my feet gave way under me. Exhausted by the day's excitement and by lack of sleep, I fell down onto the wet grass and burst into tears like a baby.

For a long time I lay motionless and cried bitterly, making no attempt to suppress the tears and sobs. I thought my lungs would burst. All my hardness and cold-bloodedness disappeared like smoke. My spirit weakened. I could not reason, and if anyone had seen me at that moment, he would have turned away in disgust.

When the night dew and the mountain wind refreshed my burning head and my thoughts were restored to their usual order, I realized it was useless and senseless to chase after a happiness that was dead. What did I need so much? To see her? Why? Was not everything over between us? One bitter kiss of farewell would not enrich my memories, and it would only make it more difficult for us to part.

However, I was pleased that I could cry. But the reason for it was probably only nerves, a sleepless night, two minutes facing the muzzle of a pistol, and an empty stomach.

It was all to the good. This new agony made a happy diversion for me, to use a military term. It is healthy to cry, and besides, if I had not ridden so far and thus had to walk the ten miles back, then sleep would probably not have closed my eyes that night either.

It was five o'clock in the morning when I returned to Kislovodsk. I threw myself onto the bed and slept the sleep of Napoleon after Waterloo.

It was dark outside when I awoke. I sat down by

the open window, unbuttoned my quilted jacket, and let the mountain wind refresh my breast, which the heavy sleep of weariness had failed to soothe. Far away, in the fort and the suburb, lights were shining through the tops of the dense limes which shaded the river. It was quiet outside, and the princess's house was dark.

The doctor came in: he was beetle-browed. He did not stretch out his hand to me as he usually did.

"Where have you come from, Doctor?"

"From Princess Ligovskoi's. Her daughter's ill—nervous prostration. But that's not why I'm here: it's this: the authorities are suspicious, and although nothing can be proved for certain, I advise you to be more careful all the same. The princess was telling me just now that she knows that you fought the duel for her daugher. That old man told her everything. What's his name? He saw your row with Grushnitski in the restaurant. I came to put you on your guard. Good-bye. Perhaps we won't meet again: they are going to send you away somewhere."

He stopped in the doorway. He wanted to shake my hand . . . and if I had displayed the least wish for it, he would have flung himself around my neck. But I remained as cold as stone—and he went out.

People are like that. They are all the same—they know all the bad aspects of an action before it is taken, but they help, advise, and even condone it, seeing the impossibility of other means. But afterward they wash their hands of it and turn away indignantly from the man who dared to assume the whole burden of responsibility. They are all the same, even the best, the cleverest.

The next morning I received an order from the high command to proceed to the fortress of I——. I called on the old princess to say good-bye.

She was surprised when to her question—did I have anything especially important to say to her?—I replied that I wished her all the best and so forth.

"But I must have a very serious talk with you."

I sat down in silence.

She obviously did not know how to begin. Her face turned rather red, her plump fingers drummed on the table. At last she began like this, in a broken voice:

"Listen, Monsieur Pechorin. I think that you are a man of honor."

I bowed.

"I am even sure of it," she continued, "though your behavior is somewhat doubtful. But you may have reasons which I don't know about, and it is these which you ought to tell me about now. You protected my daughter from slander and fought a duel for her—consequently you risked your life. Don't tell me you deny it because Grushnitski has been killed (she crossed herself), I know. God forgive him—and you too, I hope! It is no affair of mine. I cannot blame you, because although my daughter is innocent she was the cause. She told me everything . . . I think. You declared your love for her . . . she admitted her own for you (at this point the princess sighed heavily). But she is ill, and I'm sure that it's not a simple illness! A secret grief is killing her. She doesn't admit it, but I am convinced that you are the cause. Listen, perhaps you think that I am looking for rank, great wealth—nothing of the sort! I only want my daughter's happiness. Your present position is unenviable, but it can be put to right: you have a fortune; my daughter loves you, and she has been brought up to make her husband happy. I am rich; she's my only child. Tell me, what holds you back? You see, I ought not to have told you all this, but I rely on your heart, on your honor. Remember, I have one daughter . . . only one . . ."

She burst into tears.

"Princess," I said, "it's impossible for me to answer you. Let me talk to your daughter alone . . ."

"Never!" she cried, rising from her chair in a state of great agitation.

"As you will," I replied, preparing to go.

She thought for a moment, signed to me with her hand to wait, and walked out.

Five minutes passed. My heart was beating fiercely, but my thoughts were calm and my head cool. I searched my heart thoroughly for even a spark of love for the amiable Mary, but in vain.

Then the door opened and she came in. Lord! How she had changed since I last saw her—was it so long ago?

When she reached the center of the room, she began to sway. I jumped up, gave her my hand, and led her to an armchair.

I stood facing her. For a long time, neither of us said anything. Her large eyes were full of an inexpressible grief and seemed to be looking into mine for hope. Her pale lips tried in vain to smile. Her soft hands, folded on her knees, were so thin and transparent that I began to feel sorry for her.

"Princess," I said, "did you know that I have been laughing at you? You ought to despise me."

A feverish glow appeared on her cheeks.

I continued, "Consequently, you cannot love me."

She turned away, leaned on the table, and put a hand over her eyes. I thought I saw the flash of tears in them.

"My God!" she uttered, barely audibly.

It was becoming unbearable. One minute more and I would have fallen at her feet.

"And so, you can see for yourself," I said in as

firm a voice as I could muster and with a forced
sneer, "you can see for yourself that I cannot marry
you. Even if you wanted it now, you would soon
be sorry. My conversation with your mother has
forced me to explain myself openly and rudely. I
hope she is mistaken: it will be easy for you to convince her that she is. You can see for yourself that
I'm playing the most wretched and disgusting role,
I even admit it. That is all that I can do for you.
Whatever bad opinion you have of me, I shall ac-
cept it. You see, in front of you I am low. . . . Isn't
it true that even if you did love me, you despise
me from this moment?"

She turned toward me pale as marble, but her
eyes had a wonderful sparkle.

"I hate you," she said.

I thanked her, bowed respectfully, and walked
out.

In an hour an express troika was whirling me out
of Kislovodsk. A few miles from Yessentukov I saw
the corpse of my spirited horse, near the road. The
saddle had been taken—probably by a passing
Cossack—and on its back, in place of the saddle,
perched two ravens. I sighed and turned away.

And now, here in this tedious fortress, I often
ask myself as I recall the past: why did I not want
to tread that path which fate had opened up to
me? A path where quiet joys and spiritual peace
awaited me. No, I could not have survived such a
fate! I am like a sailor, born and raised on the deck
of a pirate brig. He is used to storms and battles,
and if he is thrown up on the shore, no matter how
the shady groves beckon or the peaceful sun shines
on him, he is bored and pines away. He walks all
day along the coastal sands, listening to the monotonous murmur of the incoming waves, and peers
into the misty distance. Is that not the hoped-for

sail, there on the pale line which separates the gray clouds from the dark-blue deeps? It looks like a seagull's wing at first, but, gradually it separates itself from the foam of the rollers and at even pace draws near to the empty harbor.

The Fatalist

Once, not long ago, I happened to spend two weeks at a Cossack station on our left flank. A battalion of infantry was stationed there, and in the evenings the officers would meet at each other's places in turn and play cards. On one occasion, being tired of boston and having thrown the cards under the table, we sat on a very long time at Major C.'s. The conversation was unusually absorbing. We were arguing whether the Moslem's creed, that a man's fate is written in the heavens, found many subscribers among us Christians. We all spoke of various unusual instances for and against.

"Gentlemen, all this proves nothing," said the old major: "Surely none of you has witnessed these strange happenings with which you support your opinions?"

"No, of course we haven't," many said, "but we heard of them from reliable people . . ."

"All this is nonsense," someone said. "Where are these reliable people who have seen the scroll in which the hour of our death is appointed? And if there really is predestination, then why have we been given free will, reason? Why should we account for what we do?"

At this point an officer who had been sitting in a

corner of the room got up and, walking slowly up to the table, cast a calm and triumphant glance around at everyone. He was a Serb by birth, which was obvious from his name.

Lieutenant Vulich's appearance corresponded completely with his character. The tall figure and the swarthy color of his face, the black hair, the black penetrating eyes, the large but straight nose, a characteristic of his nation, the sad, cold smile, which was always wandering over his lips—all this combined, as it were, to give him the appearance of a singular person, incapable of sharing his thoughts and passions with those whom fate had given him as comrades.

He was brave, spoke little but bitingly; entrusted his spiritual and family secrets to no one; almost never drank any wine, and never ran after the young Cossack women—whose charm is difficult to imagine without seeing them. However, it was said that the colonel's wife was not indifferent to his expressive eyes; but he would get really angry when this was hinted at.

There was only one passion which he did not conceal, a passion for cards. He would forget everything behind a green baize table; he usually lost, and continual bad luck only intensified his obstinacy. People said that one night, during an expedition, he was keeping bank on a transom and having excellent luck. Suddenly shots were fired. The alarm was sounded and everyone jumped up and rushed to arms. "Place your bet," cried Vulich, without getting up, to one of the keenest punters. "The seven will come up," replied the other as he ran out. In spite of the general confusion, Vulich completed the deal; the card came up.

There was already a fierce exchange of fire going on by the time he appeared in the line. Vulich paid no attention to the bullets or the Chechen sabers; he was trying to find his lucky punter.

"The seven came up," he shouted when he saw him at last in a line of skirmishers who were beginning to force the enemy out of the wood, and, going nearer, he took out his purse and pocketbook and handed them over to the fortunate man in spite of objections that the payment was out of place. Having fulfilled his unpleasant duty, he rushed forward, carrying the soldiers along behind him, and shot it out with the Chechens in the coolest possible way to the very end of the affair.

When Lieutenant Vulich walked up to the table, everybody stopped talking, expecting something original of him.

"Gentlemen," he said (his voice was calm although the pitch was lower than usual), "Gentlemen, what's the point of empty argument? You want proof: I suggest an experiment on myself as to whether a man dispose of his life of his own free will or whether the fatal moment is laid down in advance for each of us. . . . Who'll take me up?"

"Not I, not I," was heard on all sides. "There's a queer fellow for you. What an idea!"

"I'll take a bet with you," I said in jest.

"What are your terms?"

"I maintain that there is no predestination," I said, dropping two hundred rubles on the table, all that I had in my pocket.

"Done," replied Vulich in a sharp voice. "Major, you will be the judge. Here are a hundred and fifty rubles: you owe me the other fifty—will you do me the kindness of adding them to these."

"Very well," said the major, "but I really don't understand what it's all about. How will you decide the argument?"

Silent, Vulich went out to the major's bedroom;

we followed him. He walked up to a wall with weapons hanging on it and, at random, took one of the
various caliber pistols off its nail. We still did not
understand him, but when he cocked it and poured
powder into the touch-pan, several people could
not help crying out and taking hold of him by the
arms.

"What do you want to do? Listen, it's madness!"
they shouted at him.

"Gentlemen," he said slowly, freeing his arms,
"who will pay back the two hundred rubles for me?"

They all stopped talking and walked away.

Vulich went into the next room and sat down at
the table. We all followed him. He motioned us to
sit down around it. We obeyed him in silence. In
that moment he acquired a mysterious power over
us. I looked him steadily in the eye; he met my
searching glance with a calm and fixed look, and his
pale lips smiled. Nevertheless, in spite of his coolness, it seemed to me that I read the stamp of
death on his pale face. I have noticed—and many
old campaigners have confirmed my observation—
that there is often some sort of strange imprint of
inevitable fate on the face of a man who must die
within a few hours, which is difficult for experienced
eyes to mistake.

"You are about to die," I told him. He turned
around toward me quickly, but replied slowly and
calmly:

"Perhaps, perhaps not . . ."

Then he turned to the major and asked if the
pistol was loaded. The major, disconcerted, did not
exactly remember.

"That's enough, Vulich," someone cried, "it must
be loaded, if it was hanging at the head of the bed.
What a curious brand of humor!"

"It's a silly joke," another joined in.

"I'll bet you fifty rubles to five the pistol isn't loaded!" cried a third.

New bets were made.

This long ceremony was boring me.

"Listen," I said, "either shoot yourself, or else put the pistol back where it came from, and let's go to bed."

"Of course," many of them exclaimed, "let's go to bed."

"Gentlemen, I beg you not to move from where you are," said Vulich, putting the muzzle of the pistol to his forehead. Everyone seemed to turn to stone.

"Mister Pechorin," he continued, "turn up a card."

As I remember it now, I threw up the ace of hearts from the table; everyone stopped breathing. All eyes reflected fear and a kind of indefinable curiosity as they turned from the pistol to the ace of hearts, which quivered in the air and glided slowly down. At the very moment it touched the table, Vulich pulled the trigger . . . a misfire!

"Thank God!" exclaimed many, "it wasn't loaded . . ."

"Let's just see," said Vulich. He cocked it again, took aim at a cap which was hanging over a window; a shot rang out and the room filled with smoke. When it cleared, they took down the cap. It was pierced in the very center, and the bullet had lodged itself deep in the wall.

No one could utter a word for three minutes. Absolutely calm, Vulich poured my rubles into his purse.

People were talking about why the pistol did not shoot the first time. Some asserted that the priming pan must have been fouled, others were whispering that the powder was damp the first time and that Vulich had put in fresh afterward; but I confirmed that the latter hypothesis was unjust, for I had not taken my eyes from the pistol the whole time.

"You're a lucky gambler," I said to Vulich.

"For the first time in my life," he replied, smiling with self-satisfaction. "It's better than faro or bank!"

"But then it's rather more dangerous."

"What's that? Have you come to believe in predestination?"

"I believe in it. But now I don't understand why I thought you had to die soon."

That very man who, a short while before, had quite calmly taken aim at his own forehead, was now troubled and suddenly flared up.

"That's enough," he said, and rose to his feet; "our bet's been settled, and now your remarks strike me as being out of place . . ." He picked up his cap and walked out. I thought this odd—and not without reason.

Soon afterward everyone went off home, chatting variously about Vulich's whims and probably unanimous in calling me an egotist because I had taken up a bet with a man who wanted to commit suicide —as if he could not find a suitable opportunity without me . . .

I returned home through the deserted alleyways of the station. The moon, full and red like the glow of a fire, had begun to appear from behind a serrated skyline of houses; stars were shining calmly on the dark-blue vault, and it amused me to recall that at one time there were extremely wise people who thought that the heavenly luminaries took part in our trivial quarrels over a small plot of land or some fictitious rights. And what of it? These lamps, which, according to them, were lit solely to illuminate their own battles and triumphs, still burn with

their former luster, whereas their passions and
aspirations have long since been extinguished, together with them, like a fire lit at the edge of a wood
by a careless stranger. But at least that conviction
that the whole sky with its innumerable inhabitants
looked on them with a mute though immutable
concern gave them some power of will! . . . But we,
their pitiful descendants who wander over the earth
without convictions or pride, without pleasure or
fear—apart from the involuntary terror which grips
one's heart at the thought of the inescapable end—
we are no longer capable of great sacrifices for the
good of mankind nor even for our very own happiness, for we realize its impossibility, and so we
move indifferently from doubt to doubt—just as our
ancestors rushed from one delusion to another—
having neither hopes nor even that vague but intense
delight which the spirit gains in any struggle with
people or with fate, as they did.

Many other such thoughts arose in my mind. I
gave them free rein for I do not like to stop on any
single abstract thought; what does it lead to? In my
early youth I was a dreamer; I loved to linger over
the somber and the optimistic forms which arose
in turn in my restless imagination. But what did it
leave me with? Only a weariness like that which
follows a night-long struggle with ghosts, and con-
fused recollections full of regrets. In this vain battle
I exhausted both the heat of my spirit and the constancy of my will, which is essential to a real life. I
entered on this life having already lived it in my
thoughts, and I became bored and disgusted, like
one who reads a poor imitation of a book he has
known for a long time.

The incident that evening had made quite a deep
impression on me and had frayed my nerves. I do
not know for certain now whether I believed in

predestination or not, but I believed in it firmly that evening. The evidence was striking, and although I had been laughing at our ancestors and their obliging astrology, I had slipped unconsciously into their tracks; but I stopped myself in time on that dangerous road, and holding the principle of dismissing nothing completely and believing blindly in nothing, I cast out metaphyics and began to come down to earth. This precaution was very relevant for I almost fell down, having bumped into something fat and soft and obviously inanimate. I bent down—the moon was shining straight on the road —and what did I see? In front of me lay a pig slashed in half by a saber. . . . I hardly had time to take a good look at it before I heard the noise of footsteps: two Cossacks were running out of an alleyway; one came up to me and asked if I had seen a drunken Cossack chasing a pig. I told him I had not met the Cossack, and pointed to the unfortunate victim of his rabid high spirits.

"What a ruffian," said the second Cossack. "He gets drunk on unfermented wine and goes off to chop up everything he finds. Let's get after him, Yeremyeich. We must tie him up, or else . . ."

They went off, and I continued on my way with great caution and happily reached my quarters at last.

I was living with an old Cossack sergeant whom I liked for his kind disposition and particularly for his pretty daughter, Nastya.

As usual she was waiting for me at the gate wrapped up in a fur coat; the moon was shining on her pretty lips which had turned bluish from the night cold. She smiled when she saw me, but I was not in the mood for her. "Good night, Nastya," I said as I went past. She wanted to say something in reply, but only sighed.

I closed the door of my room behind me, lit a candle, and threw myself onto the bed, but this time sleep kept me waiting longer than usual. The east was already beginning to grow pale by the time I fell asleep, but I was obviously fated not to sleep well that night. At four o'clock in the morning two fists banged on my window. I jumped up: what was the matter?

"Get up, get dressed!" several voices shouted to me. I dressed hurriedly and went out. "Do you know what's happened?" three officers said to me in one voice as they came in for me; they were as white as death.

"What?"

"Vulich has been killed."

I was stunned.

"Yes, killed," they continued. "Let's get there quickly."

"But where?"

"You'll find out on the way."

We set off. They told me everything that had happened, with an admixture of various comments about the strange fate which had saved him from inevitable death half an hour before he died. Vulich was walking alone along a dark street; the drunken Cossack who had slashed the pig ran up and might perhaps have gone past without noticing him if Vulich had not stopped suddenly and said, "Whom are you looking for, old chap?"

"You," answered the Cossack, striking him with the saber and cutting him through from the shoulder almost to the heart. The two Cossacks who had met me and were following the murderer rushed up and lifted the injured man, but he was already at his last gasp and said only three words: "He was right!" Only I understood the dark import of these words: they referred to me. Involuntarily I had told the poor fellow of his fate; my instinct had not deceived me; I had read the signs of near death on his changed face accurately.

The murderer had shut himself up in an empty hovel on the outskirts of the station: we were going there. A crowd of women were running, weeping, in the same direction; now and then a Cossack who been left behind would jump onto the road, hurriedly belting on his dagger, and outstrip us at a run. The confusion was frightful.

We arrived there at last to see a crowd around the hovel whose doors and shutters were bolted from inside. Officers and Cossacks were talking heatedly among themselves; women were wailing, chanting, and lamenting. I caught sight of a significant face among them—that of an old woman—which reflected an insane despair. She was sitting on a thick log, resting her elbows on her knees and supporting her head with her hands: it was the murderer's mother. Her lips moved from time to time: was it a prayer or a curse that they whispered?

Meanwhile some way had to be found to capture the offender. However, no one dared to be the first to rush in.

I went up to the window and took a look through a chink in the shutter: pale, he was lying on the floor holding a pistol in his right hand; a blood-bespattered saber lay near him. His expressive eyes were rotating with fright; now and again he shuddered and clasped his head, as if recalling vaguely what had happened during the night. I did not see any great determination in that troubled look and told the major that there was no point in his not having the door broken down and rushing in some Cossacks, for it was better to do that now, rather than later when he had collected himself completely.

At that moment an old captain of Cossacks went

up to the door and called him by his name: the man shouted back.

"You have sinned, brother Yefimich," said the Cossack captain, "so there's nothing for it. Give yourself up."

"I won't surrender," replied the Cossack.

"Have some fear of God! You're not a damned Chechen, but an honest Christian, aren't you? It can't be helped if your sin's muddled your head. You can't escape your fate."

"I won't give myself up!" cried the Cossack threateningly, and one could hear the click as he cocked the gun.

"Hey, Auntie," said the Cossack captain to the old woman, "talk to your son—perhaps he'll listen to you. . . . All this is only angering God. And look, these gentlemen here have been waiting here for two hours already."

The old woman looked at him fixedly and shook her head.

"Vasilly Petrovich," said the captain of Cossacks, walking up to the major, "he won't surrender—I know him; and if the door's broken down, he'll get a lot of our men. Wouldn't it be better for you to have him shot? There's a wide chink in the shutter."

At that moment a strange thought entered my mind. Like Vulich, I had the idea of testing fate.

"Wait," I told the major. "I'll get him alive."

Bidding the captain of Cossacks to hold him in conversation and placing three Cossacks by the door, ready to break it down and rush to my aid at a given signal, I walked around the hut and approached a side window. My heart was beating fiercely.

"Oh, you heathen," cried the Cossack captain, "what, are you laughing at us? Do you think we won't get you?" He started to bang on the door with all his might. I put my eye to the chink and followed the Cossack's movements but he was not expecting an attack from that side, and suddenly I tore the shutter open and dived headlong through the window. A shot rang out just above my ear, and the bullet tore off an epaulette. But the smoke which filled the room kept my adversary from finding the saber which was lying near him. I grabbed him by the arms; the Cossacks broke in and in less than three minutes the culprit was tied up and taken away under escort. The crowd broke up and the officers congratulated me—and, really, not for nothing.

How could one not become a fatalist after all this? But who knows if he is really convinced of something or not? . . . How frequently we take a sensory deception, or a miscalculation, for a conviction. I prefer to doubt everything. This frame of mind does not hamper a resolute disposition; on the contrary, as far as I am concerned, I always go forward more bravely when I do not know what is waiting for me. Why, nothing worse than death ever happens—and one cannot escape death!

Returning to the fort, I told Maxim everything that had happened to me and that I had seen, wishing to learn his opinion about predestination. At first he did not understand this word, but I explained it to him as best I could and then he said with a significant shake of his head:

"Yes, sir, of course! This is quite a difficult point! . . . But then, these Asiatic flintlocks often misfire if they're badly greased or if you don't press your finger quite hard enough. I don't like Circassian rifles either, I must say: they're not right somehow for the likes of us; they've got small butts —before you know where you are you've burned your nose off . . . but then I have the highest respect for their swords!"

Then, having pondered a little, he added:

"Yes, I feel sorry for the poor chap. . . . The devil must have got into him for him to talk to a drunkard at night! . . . But then it's clear that it was decreed thus at his birth! . . ."

I could not get anything more out of him; he does not care for metaphysical debates at all.

Translator's Note

     This translation was based on the text contained in the collected edition of Lermontov's works published in Moscow in 1958, which in turn follows the corrected second edition of 1841. I have aimed at an accurate version with no abridgements, though I have expanded and contracted a phrase occasionally in order to reflect the emphasis of the Russian. I have made no attempt to rhyme the verse, though I hope it gives some impression of the original meter. Fortunately Lermontov was not lavish in the use of patronymics, and most of such few as occur I have been bold enough to leave out. I have translated the few Turkish words that appear in the original, but left in French phrases placed with psychological intent and impact in the original dialogue. Military terms have been rendered by the nearest current English equivalent and measurements converted, but Russian monetary expressions have been left as they are.

P. L.

Afterword

Mikhail Yurevich Lermontov (1814-1841) was born the son of a poor army officer and a wealthy heiress. The boy's mother died when he was only three, and the maternal grandmother secured custody of the child. She provided him with a comfortable upbringing and a good education. Lermontov was a precocious youth and had free access to the large family library. He read voraciously, including Schiller's *The Robbers* and some poems of Byron, works that undoubtedly influenced his own extravagant romanticism.

The boy grew up shy and awkard, ashamed of his appearance: he was stoop-shouldered and a bit bow-legged. He cultivated a cynical wit and a sense of irony to protect himself from the taunts of those about him. It is noteworthy that in an unpublished fragment Pechorin is described as ugly, too.

In 1830 Lermontov entered the University of Moscow, but two years later he transferred to the University and then the cavalry school in St. Petersburg. In 1834, in spite of his rather unruly behavior as a cadet, he was awarded a commission as an officer in the Hussars.

Lermontov had been writing poetry since the age

of thirteen, including some rather pornographic verses in cadet school. After the death of the great Russian poet Pushkin in a duel in 1837 Lermontov wrote a vehement denunciation in verse of the authorities who had persecuted Pushkin and allowed him to perish. The poem was not published but received a wide circulation in manuscript. Someone sent a copy to Tsar Nicholas I, who promptly exiled Lermontov to duty in the Caucasus. En route to this assignment, the young officer stopped in the seaport of Taman and became involved with a band of smugglers, an adventure that almost cost him his life but that later served as the basis for "Taman." Transfer to another regiment within a year permitted Lermontov to return to the capital, where he found his literary reputation established. A quarrel with the son of the French ambassador led to a duel and his second arrest, and the Tsar ordered him back to the Caucasus. His grandmother soon managed to obtain leave for him; however, the authorities were displeased by his return to Petersburg, and three months later he was sent back to service in the Caucasus; strict orders were issued to keep him in the front lines—virtually a death sentence.

The poet frustrated the Tsar's order by stopping off in Pyatigorsk, where he had himself put on the sick list and plunged into the social life of the fashionable Caucasian spa. But he soon quarreled with an old schoolmate, Major Martynov, whose dandified airs were a natural target for Lermontov's acid wit. Inevitably a challenge was issued, and the duel was staged in the manner of the Grushnitski-Pechorin duel in "Princess Mary." Lermontov either fired in the air or did not fire at all; Martynov killed his opponent with a single shot. Thus fate provided an ironic reversal of the outcome of the fictional encounter, where Pechorin, the Lermontov-like hero, kills the dandified Grushnitski.

The Caucasus became a favorite setting for Russian writers with the publication of Pushkin's narrative poem "A Prisoner of the Caucasus" in 1822. Wild and craggy, it was a land of snow-capped peaks and savage mountain tribesmen. Russia had annexed the Christian Kingdom of Georgia in 1801. Separated by the main range of the Caucasus Mountains, the two lands lacked a common border. This and the need to protect the settlers in the valleys from periodic raids led the Tsarist government to undertake a war against the mountain tribesmen. The war lasted, with interruptions, for more than fifty years. Three generations of Russians, the last two represented by Lermontov and Tolstoy, were involved in the campaign. The Caucasus held a double fascination for these writers: it was a land of magnificent, rugged scenery, and it was the dwelling place of primitive tribesmen whose life was a ready source of exotic material. Rousseauistic Romanticism, the belief that savages are nobler and more honest than civilized men, is a marked tenet of the Russian "Caucasian writers": Pushkin's "Prisoner," Lermontov's *Mtsyri*, and Tolstoy's *The Cossacks*, three works that cover a span of more than forty years and that differ greatly in style and technique, all share this view. So do the exotic novels of Alexander Bestuzhev-Marlinsky (1797-1837), a nobleman who was sentenced to serve in the ranks for his part in the Decembrist Uprising of 1825. Marlinsky's novels, with their labored scenes of society and forced wit, served as a model for *A Hero of Our Time*.

Though Lermontov's novel is in the Byronic tradition and is set in the Caucasus, it contains

relatively little "local color": there are a few evoca-
tions of the region in "Bela" and a few landscape
scenes in "Princess Mary" (along with a description
of Pechorin's riding costumes), but even these
"exotic" elements do not appear entirely free of
irony. In *A Hero of Our Time* Lermontov was clearly moving away from the novel of adventure toward
an intense social and psychological study. Had he
not died, prematurely, at the age of twenty-seven,
there is evidence that he would have continued
working in this direction.

Lermontov's other writings are uneven, partly
because of his extreme youth. His lyric poems alter-
nate a cynical demonism with occasional dreams of
a lost paradise of angelic bliss. *Mtsyri* (1840), a
long narrative poem, depicts a young man's struggle
to escape the confines of civilization and find freedom for himself in his native land. But he is too
weak for the struggle and, in the end, perishes. *The
Demon,* completed in 1839 after many revisions but
never published in the author's lifetime, remains an
imperfect work. Its subject, the struggle of a fallen
angel to redeem himself from the tedium of his
existence through the love of a mortal maiden, seems
patently ridiculous today. Yet the poem, like the
best of Lermontov's lyrics, contains superb landscape scenes along with an intense and passionate
rhetoric.

Lermontov's earlier prose attempts are mere frag-
ments. *Vadim* is an uncompleted historical novel of
the eighteenth-century Pugachov Rebellion, a subject also treated by Pushkin in his novel *The Captain's Daughter* (1836). Also uncompleted is *The
Princess Ligovskoy,* which introduces the figure of
Pechorin, already recognizably similar to the hero
of the later novel.

Lermontov first published *A Hero of Our Time* in book form in 1840. Of the five episodes that make up the novel, three—"Bela," "The Fatalist," and "Taman"—had been published as separate stories a year earlier in the journal *The Fatherland Notes*. Biographical information on the circumstances of the novel's composition is inadequate to determine whether Lermontov conceived the plan of the cycle from the beginning, or whether the idea of uniting the stories into a novel occurred to him only in the course of his work. Certain rather obvious inconsistencies suggest that the stories do not add up to a unified whole. Pechorin, who is later to appear in "Princess Mary" and "The Fatalist" as a romantic superman who overcomes all obstacles and whom it is impossible to outwit, is himself pitifully outwitted in "Taman."

On the other hand, certain internal parallels and symmetries suggest that the novel was planned as a unified whole and not just a collection of tales. Both "Bela" and "Taman" deal with the Romantic's dream of finding happiness in the love of a primitive girl, and the disillusionment of that dream. At the same time Pechorin's three affairs with Bela, Vera, and Princess Mary all show the futility of love, at least for him.

The reader is struck by the obvious tension between the chronological order in which the stories occur and the order in which they are presented by the author. The earliest in time of occurrence is "Taman," followed rather closely by "Princess Mary." The Russian critic Eichenbaum, the leading authority on Lermontov, places "Bela" next in order, but in fact the sequence of "The Fatalist" and "Bela" is unclear. Both occur during the year Pechorin spends with Maxim Maximich in the "Fortress of N." We are told that Pechorin reports for duty in autumn and leaves in December of the following year. In "The Fatalist" the daughter of Pechorin's host wears a fur coat at night, suggesting an autumn or winter setting, while the action of "Bela," which lasts some months, takes place over the spring and summer. Thus "The Fatalist" might have occurred either before or after "Bela," either soon after Pechorin's original arrival at the fortress, or not long before his departure. Most likely Lermontov himself was little concerned with precise chronology, and did not bother to work it out in detail. Finally, "Maxim Maximich" takes place last of all, some five years after "Bela."

The diversity of narrators and the presence of certain minor inconsistencies among the different episodes, as well as the fact of earlier publication of three of them as separate and complete tales—all this suggests that the finished work is only a cycle of tales united around a common character, and not a novel. Add to this the fact that the presentation and analysis of Pechorin's character come to a proper end in "Princess Mary"; the final story, "The Fatalist," though absorbing, sheds no new light on Pechorin and seems somehow "left over." The placing of "The Fatalist" at the end suggests that Lermontov had in mind taking more stories from Pechorin's journal for a sequel—in fact he had promised to do just that for the events of Pechorin's earlier life in Petersburg—here he may have been thinking of his own unfinished *Princess Ligovskoy*.

But still there are important grounds for considering the work as a novel. The subject is a single one: the revelation of Pechorin's character, presented first as an enigma, but then analyzed and to a degree

interpreted. The variety of narrative points of view
in the different stories is deliberate and controlled.
Pechorin's strange inability to love is first remarked
upon by a naïve observer, Maxim Maximich, who
does not and cannot comprehend Pechorin. The
tension between Maxim's narrative and the narrative of the "neutral" author, the man writing the
travel sketch that frames Maxim's narrative, creates
irony but only compounds the enigma by prolong-
ing the narrative. For the time being Pechorin himself is kept "off stage," like many a melodramatic
figure, to increase suspense. In the next story we
confront him directly—Lermontov even provides a
good physical description of his hero but the encounter is too brief to do more than impress us with
his dramatic intensity. Finally, in "Princess Mary"
we penetrate to his very soul as he sees and analyzes
it himself. Lermontov would hardly have been disturbed by the possible objection that his final terms
are subjective, for as a Romanticist he plainly pre-
ferred subjective analysis—Pechorin was, after all,
in a certain sense a projection of himself. Moreover,
the novel told in the first person gives a sense of
intimacy and familiarity, as well as intensity, which
can hardly be achieved in a third-person narrative.
It is noteworthy that novels revolving around a
single figure are so often narrated in the first person,
from Goethe and Constant through Dickens down to
Proust and Camus.

The form of the novel thus combines two conflicting principles: melodramatic suspense, built
around the enigma of Pechorin's coldness, and self-
revelation, in which the enigma is exposed and laid
open by self-analysis. The conflict of the two principles results in a novel that has progressive
phases: the reader first sees Pechorin at a great

distance, through the eyes of others, but gradually moves in on him, like a motion picture camera closing in on a scene. The novel is in fact a whole, in which we have a single subject, the analysis of Pechorin's character. The problem is stated in "Bela," amplified in "Maxim Maximich," and finally resolved in "Princess Mary." "Taman" is a brief interlude of atmospheric character, a digression permissible within the relatively loose structure of the novel. Only "The Fatalist" evades the pattern of the structure; it might better have been placed earlier, except that in a total of only five tales, two interludes would have been excessive, and the reader's suspense would have been dissipated. In its present position at the end of the book it becomes an anticlimax.

As an exaggerated Romantic hero, Pechorin might have been taken for a parody, particularly since the tradition of the Byronic hero was already a long-established one. As Eichenbaum has remarked, Lermontov avoids this danger by creating a living parody of Pechorin—Grushnitski—whose dandified manners, feeble wit, and exaggerated ennui are all assumed, largely with an eye toward the ladies. Pechorin in fact sees Grushnitski as a parody of himself and therefore hates him. But the contrast provides the partial illusion that Pechorin has the noble characteristics of the Byronic hero, Grushnitski the baser ones. Also related to Pechorin is Dr. Werner, who, like Grushnitski, serves as a sounding-board for Pechorin's epigrams. But there is a certain suggestion (though it is not developed with entire consistency) that Werner resembles Pechorin in his estrangement from society but surpasses him in his detachment: love and hatred have become equally boring for him.

Russian criticism, both tsarist and Soviet, followed the leftist critic Dobrolyubov's meaningful but overdrawn generalization that Russian heroes are "superfluous men," and so emphasized the theme of social and political opposition in the novel. Of course, neither political nor social criticism appears in the book as we have it, and the Russian censorship of the day would not have permitted it. Lermontov's criticism, then, must be considered to be implicit. In this view, Pechorin is estranged from a society that denies him a proper outlet for his talents, his dynamic energy, and his liberally inclined spirit. Frustrated, he becomes an army officer, one of the few "respectable" careers open to him as a member of the landed gentry. But the army bores him and gives him no ideal worth fighting for. Stultified by a reactionary society Pechorin's energies become destructive.

The argument is plausible, but it errs by attributing to Lermontov the views of a later generation. Lermontov hardly made a distinction between reaction as such and mere philistinism, or between society as a source of power and approval and society as a set of disagreeable prejudices and manners. Both were symptomatic of the society he hated. If Pechorin is estranged from his own society, he would presumably have been estranged from any society. Nor is there any evidence to show that Lermontov had very strong liberal or reform convictions, or that he associated with liberals as a matter of preference. It is curious that he deliberately avoided most of the writers of his own generation, including those with progressive tendencies.

Eichenbaum makes much of the fact that a draft version of the novel refers to a duel as the cause of Pechorin's exile from St. Petersburg to the Caucasus (this was presumably written before Lermontov's duel with the son of the French ambassador led to his own exile there!). But a duel is usually not political, and we can hardly claim that the detail is anything more than a romantic cliché intended to endow Pechorin with a mysterious and intriguing past.

Stronger is the suggestion implicit in the novel's title that Pechorin is a typical figure of the era. This conception is actually derived from the title of a novel by Alfred de Musset, *The Confession of a Child of the Century* (1836), and Lermontov may just as well have meant the European post-Napoleonic and late Romantic generations as the Russian generation that experienced the tyranny of the reign of Nicholas I. Nor is Pechorin "typical" in any statistical sense: in fact, he is set off against every other character in the novel. Both Lermontov and Pechorin were estranged from their worlds, and there is considerable irony implicit in the novel's title.

Pechorin has many antecedents in Romantic literature, as the reader is no doubt well aware. The jejune hero, hopelessly at variance with the society about him, who may strike back at society for its cruelty and indifference to him, had already been drawn in Schiller's *The Robbers* (1781), in Chateaubriand's *René* (1802), and the heroes of Byron. A more immediate model is the hero of Musset's *"Confession,"* published only a few years before Lermontov's novel. Nor did Lermontov introduce the type to Russian literature; Pushkin's Eugene Onegin is an earlier example of a jaded, alienated Byronic hero on Russian soil. Lermontov calls Pechorin "a hero of our time," but it might be more accurate to describe him as the hero of a generation that was already passing from the scene. The realistic novel swept onto the stage soon after 1840, and in Russian social and economic philosophy the code of a Romantic idealism was beginning to give way to a new pragmatic and businesslike ethic, of the sort advocated in Goncharov's novel *A Common Story* (1847). In fact, the early realists, such as Turgenev and Goncharov, were Lermontov's exact contemporaries.

One could hardly deny that Pechorin (and to a degree Lermontov) were, in the terms of modern psychology, narcissistic and neurotic. Pechorin's inability to love, his failure to turn his great gifts to any but petty ends, his manipulative, opportunistic, at times even vindictive treatment of his fellow men and, even more, women, would all suggest narcissism and even sadism. To be sure, these traits are rendered more savory by combining them with other characteristics of the Romantic hero, more socially acceptable if equally narcissistic: exaggerated courage to the point of indifference to death; the glamour of the *homme fatal* whom no woman can resist; the possession of leadership and talent rarely put to any use except in military action, adventure, or seduction. The type is in a sense self-contradictory: heroism and neurosis, sensitivity to injustice and callous indifference to the suffering of others, love of feminine beauty and narcissistic self-adoration. Yet such men are at least occasionally found in real life, and in literature the type has been a perennial favorite, even outside the Romantic era. Dickens' Steerforth, Stendhal's Julien Sorel, and Dostoevsky's Stavrogin are all later examples, not to mention countless heroes of detective and adventure fiction. All these characters are, in a sense, children of the Romantic Movement; even the existentialist hero of our own times comes from the same family. Camus' Stranger, as a typical man of our own day, lacks the aristocratic pose, the glamour and sexual attractiveness characteristic of the Byronic hero, but he retains many other traits of the type and their paradoxical intermixture. The ennui of the Byronic hero remains, but it is transformed into bottomless, even principled indifference and is employed to punish an irrational universe much as the Romantic hero's ennui and hostility were visited on an indifferent world.

Pechorin has something of the quality of the existentialist hero; thus he is in a sense a hero of *our* time as well. Pechorin is not bored—he is in fact highly intrigued by his own machinations—but he is profoundly indifferent. He tells us that in the final analysis he does not know why he acts as he does, why he flirts with Princess Mary, why he tortures her, why he does not and cannot marry her. Rather than regarding himself as a rational being alone in an irrational world, as a purely narcissistic hero might have done, Pechorin acknowledges, in spite of his contempt for others, that there is no real distinction between his own behavior and the world's; the difference lies only in his flair for success and in the extent of his self-consciousness. He does not, for the most part, attempt to rationalize the evil he does; he simply does it as a gratuitous symptom of ultimate irrationality, like Camus' Stranger, who kills the Arab for no more definable reason than that the weather is very hot. The beautiful metaphor that closes "Princess Mary," the image of the sail appearing on the distant horizon, a symbol of Pechorin's yearning after his own fate, may be taken as Romantic nostalgia for loneliness and death, but it may also be interpreted as the sense of existentialist freedom that rewards Pechorin's search for self-definition through self-isolation and the performance of evil, almost criminal acts. Though "Bela" appealed most to the taste of Lermontov's contemporaries, and "Taman" to the mood-loving Chekhov, it is "Princess Mary," decidedly, that has most to say to us today, and structurally it is the true heart and climax of the novel.

The influence of Lermontov's novel on later Russian literature was considerable. To be sure, the end of the Romantic era made direct imitation unfashionable, and it is rather criticism of Pechorin and what he stands for that concerns the early realists. Thus, in his *Sevastopol Sketches* (1855-56), Tolstoy parodies the image of the proud aristocratic officer who pretends to feel no fear, and through this parody he hits at all romantic self-dramatization and empty posing. For Tolstoy the men who fight bravely and who win the battles are not the foppish amateurs, but the professional soldiers, men who trace their lineage back, not to Pechorin, but to Maxim Maximich. On the other hand, both Tolstoy's Prince Andrey (in *War and Peace*) and Dostoevsky's Stavrogin (in *The Possessed*) are in the tradition of the Byronic hero in general and Pechorin in particular.

What is more significant, however, is the element of psychological analysis that Lermontov made so prominent in his novel. Earlier Russian prose had eschewed psychologizing almost with positive mistrust; thus Pushkin's "Tales of Belkin" are pure romantic narratives, free from analysis of motivation or inner conflicts, without any real character development. Lermontov gives us all three of these elements of novelistic analysis. To be sure, he is hardly ahead of his time in his psychology, and we cannot look to him for the kind of prefiguring of Freudian ideas we have come to expect in Dostoevsky. But Lermontov created, almost alone, a Russian novel in which the psychology of the hero played the major role; it was with this example in mind that the great masters of Russian fiction, Turgenev, Dostoevsky, and Tolstoy, went on to explore more profound psychological depths.

WILLIAM E. HARKINS
Columbia University.

NEL BESTSELLERS

Science Fiction

T014 576	THE INTERPRETER	Brian Aldiss	30p
T015 017	EQUATOR	Brian Aldiss	30p
T014 347	SPACE RANGER	Isaac Asimov	30p
T015 491	PIRATES OF THE ASTEROIDS	Isaac Asimov	30p
T019 780	THROUGH A GLASS CLEARLY	Isaac Asimov	30p
T020 673	MOONS OF JUPITER	Isaac Asimov	35p
T011 631	MASTER MIND OF MARS	Edgar Rice Burroughs	30p
T015 564	LOST ON VENUS	Edgar Rice Burroughs	35p
T010 333	REVOLT IN 2100	Robert Heinlein	40p
T021 602	THE MAN WHO SOLD THE MOON	Robert Heinlein	40p
T016 900	STRANGER IN A STRANGE LAND	Robert Heinlein	75p
T022 862	DUNE	Frank Herbert	80p
T012 298	DUNE MESSIAH	Frank Herbert	40p
T015 211	THE GREEN BRAIN	Frank Herbert	30p

War

T013 367	DEVIL'S GUARD	Robert Elford	50p
T020 584	THE GOOD SHEPHERD	C. S. Forester	40p
T011 755	TRAWLERS GO TO WAR	Lund & Ludlam	40p
T012 999	P.Q.17—CONVOY TO HELL	Lund & Ludlam	30p
T014 215	THE GIANT KILLERS	Kenneth Poolman	40p
T022 528	THE LAST VOYAGE OF GRAF SPEE	Michael Powell	35p

Western

T016 994	No. 1 EDGE—THE LONER	George G. Gilman	30p
T016 986	No. 2 EDGE—TEN THOUSAND DOLLAR AMERICAN	George G. Gilman	30p
T017 613	No. 3 EDGE—APACHE DEATH	George G. Gilman	30p
T017 001	No. 4 EDGE—KILLER'S BREED	George G. Gilman	30p
T016 536	No. 5 EDGE—BLOOD ON SILVER	George G. Gilman	30p
T017 621	No. 6 EDGE—THE BLUE THE GREY AND THE RED	George G. Gilman	30p
T014 479	No. 7 EDGE—CALIFORNIA KILLING	George G. Gilman	30p
T015 254	No. 8 EDGE—SEVEN OUT OF HELL	George G. Gilman	30p
T015 475	No. 9 EDGE—BLOODY SUMMER	George G. Gilman	30p
T015 769	No. 10 EDGE—VENGEANCE IS BLACK	George G. Gilman	30p
T017 184	No. 11 EDGE—SIOUX UPRISING	George G. Gilman	30p
T017 893	No. 12 EDGE—THE BIGGEST BOUNTY	George G. Gilman	30p
T018 253	No. 13 EDGE—A TOWN CALLED HATE	George G. Gilman	30p
T020 754	No. 14 EDGE—THE BIG GOLD	George G. Gilman	30p

General

T021 009	SEX MANNERS FOR MEN	Robert Chartham	35p
T019 403	SEX MANNERS FOR ADVANCED LOVERS	Robert Chartham	30p
W002 835	SEX AND THE OVER FORTIES	Robert Chartham	30p
T010 732	THE SENSUOUS COUPLE	Dr. 'C'	25p

Mad

S004 892	MAD MORALITY		40p
S005 172	MY FRIEND GOD		40p
S005 069	MAD FOR BETTER OR VERSE		30p

NEL, P.O. BOX 11, FALMOUTH, TR10 9EN, CORNWALL

Please send cheque or postal order. Allow 10p to cover postage and packing on one book plus 5p for each additional book.

Name..

Address ....

....

Title..
(NOVEMBER)